Grand Pacifica

Grand Pacifica

Brent Stephen Smith

This is a work of fiction. All names, characters, places, and incidents are a product of the author's imagination. Any resemblance to real events or persons, living or dead, is entirely coincidental.

Copyright © 2012 Brent Stephen Smith

ISBN: 978-0-9810752-7-3

First edition

Brent Stephen Smith
brentstephensmith@gmail.com
brentstephensmith.wordpress.com

September 11, 2001

"Looks like the world is ending."

I said the words with a small amount of humour as my best friend, Sergey, walked towards me, expressionless. We had made wild exclamatory statements before, but something seemed off about it this time. There was more than a hint of truth to it. That bite sunk deep into our skins and festered. We had never been so shocked. His face was pale and his eyes met me as if a profundity had awoken in him.

I woke that morning the same as always. I was sixteen and it was the beginning of the school year. Waking the same as always meant arguing with myself about the value of dragging my weary body out of bed or lying around much longer and letting my face feel the cool embrace of a newly flipped over pillow. Finding any interest in going to school usually came down to whether I had any pillows left to flip. It seems arbitrary, but then most decisions in life are. I could have decided to lie in bed much longer and my innocence would have rested with me there, if only for a few hours more. I don't know when it would happen, maybe around noon, when I finally get up and put a pot on the stove, boiling water to cook macaroni and cheese, and I turn the television on, hoping to watch some trash. It would happen then. I'd see our future.

It didn't happen that way. I think so, anyways. What I remember was different. I remember getting up, having lost my battle with a warm pillow, and pouring a bowl of cereal. I sat at the kitchen table and stared at the wall. That sounds dumb, but the wall was actually covered in tiled mirrors. That sounds vain. Maybe it was. In any case, I sat at the table, looking at myself, eating cereal when the phone rang. My sister, Ashley, grabbed the phone before I could. To be fair, she noticed the phone ringing before I did. She noticed the phone before I noticed her. I remember that mirrored wall so well, but I forget these details. Was she at the table with me? Possibly. Where was Dad? Dad was also sitting at the table, drinking coffee. I don't know if he was drinking coffee, but Dad liked to drink coffee every morning, so it would figure in this recreation that he would be drinking some then. He probably was eating toast with peanut butter, too.

Mom wasn't there. That I remember. I remember that part because Mom was on the phone with Ashley. Or was it Dad who answered the phone? I think it was Ashley. Ashley answered the phone.

"Hello?"

"Ashley, turn on the T.V."

"Sorry?"

"Turn on the T.V., Ashley."

"Mom wants us to turn on the T.V."

"What channel?"

"What channel, Mom?"

"Any channel."

Then it became clear. There had been a horrible accident. A plane had crashed into a building in New York City. It was awful to hear. It was mind-boggling to watch. But then more happened. More planes. More buildings. The Pentagon. Some place in Pennsylvania. Terrorists. Jihadists, apparently. I didn't know the word Jihad. It's become more familiar since.

We watched the news anchors try to explain the situation. They failed. It was too hard to comprehend. Of all the 5Ws of news reporting, it was unclear the answer to the one everyone wanted to know most – why?

Why would anyone willingly take over a plane just to crash it into a building? Who could really see that as being a solution to whatever problems they have? It made no sense. Even if you were fighting the Jihad, wouldn't it make more sense to live? You can fight more battles if you are alive than if you die in a single battle.

In that high school hallway, painted beige and green (or was it still blue, then?), I looked at Sergey and tried to understand what had just happened to our lives. Was it really the end times? Spelled with capitals for emphasis and doom: was it really the End Times?

"I think so."

"What?"

"I think you're right. I think the world is ending."

"Man, I thought we'd get a longer run."

I don't know if I actually made a pithy comment like that. It's something that in retrospect I may have added. It could have been like a director's cut DVD (remember those?) where they add in things they wish were there originally, but didn't make the final version of the movie. Maybe it was more like the outtakes and additional commentary. In any case, I can't remember that part all that well.

It was such a shock. It came as such a shock. There could have been nothing more shocking that could have happened at that point in my life. What would our educators tell us? What would they do to calm the young and impressionable minds that had just seen four planes fly directly into their minds? This is a teachable moment. This is when elders can impart all the lessons of the past to fill the youth with the knowledge and ability to carry us forward. We were the future, remember? I believed that. I believed that I was being groomed to make a difference. There would be a time later in life when things I learned as a teenager would allow me to make my mark on the world. I was so foolish.

"This is a direct result of American foreign policy."

You had to love the way that Mr. Franks didn't avoid the truth. It came out of his mouth early enough and in a quiet enough way that I don't think he ever received backlash. He didn't have to worry about sponsors pulling out of his late night program. He didn't have to worry about getting re-elected. Mr. Franks was a public school history teacher and his only job was to educate. He decided to educate us in the tit for tat manner of international affairs. His view was quite simple: that the imperialistic United States of America had spent far too many years expanding themselves into far too many places and had pissed off far too many people. Due to this expansion of empire, Uncle Sam was bound to receive backlash. This backlash happened all the time, but it never really struck a chord with the general American public because it happened overseas. Enter the events of September 11th, where a small group of Islamic extremists decided to hijack four planes with box cutters in order to make a statement on American soil. Mission: Accomplished.

In the short days that followed, that honest assessment would come from Mr. Franks and Mr. Franks alone. Watching the American twenty-four hour news channels provided nothing close to a similar view. A wild hysteria of patriotism and fervent nationalism sprouted up instead. If you didn't know that American symbols of freedom involved stars and stripes, well you were sure to know during that period of jingoistic grandstanding. If the Jihadists hated America before, they must have really hated America after.

"Mr. Franks says that it is because of American foreign policy."

"Yeah, soldiers in Mecca."

"U.S. support of Israel."

"Crass consumerism."

"Hubris."

I don't know if we knew half of those words. I don't know if we said half of them. It's all become a blur, because the world events that followed seemed to swallow that day up. I think we may have had some announcement from the principal. There might have been an offer of counseling. I don't know if that happened or not, but I remember something like that being offered after Columbine. That was my generation, I think now. The Columbine generation. The generation that watched in disbelief. When I thought I lost my innocence the morning of September 11th, maybe I was wrong. It must have been a few years earlier, with Columbine. Or did it come even earlier? Was innocence something I lost all at once, with one fell swoop, or was it something that came with a thousand cuts over time?

One thousand cuts over time. Wow, could it be? Could it be true? What was the opposite of innocence? Maybe instead of losing innocence, we gain the opposite. It just keeps getting stacked up, over and over again, until we are each these towers of experience and cynicism.

My mind keeps going back to that moment of shock. I remember watching the television replay the image of a plane flying into the side of the World Trade Center. I remember seeing the smoke come from the side of the building. I remember the building fall. I remember the repeat. Plane flying. World Trade Center hit. Smoke from side. Falling building. Repeat. Plane. Center. Smoke. Fall. Repeat. It looped over and over, a spool of horror.

Every other detail, whether Ashley was at the table with me, or whether Dad was eating toast with peanut butter just seems so inconsequential to what was such a defining moment in my young life. The mind struggles to recall all the minutiae, but it has no difficulties with the major facts of consequence. I know that the World Trade Center was hit that day. I saw the plane. I saw the smoke. I saw the crumble. I don't feel like examining the conspiracies that say it looked more like a controlled implosion. They've looked at the video over and over again, looking for small details that miss the big picture. The big picture is important. Those planes hit those towers. Dad may have been eating a grapefruit.

There is a fuzz, a haze really, that hangs around that day at school. I don't recall any other class but Mr. Franks' history class. Why is it that on such a historical occasion, the only class I can really remember is Mr. Franks' history class? I can't even recall what other classes I was taking that semester. Chemistry? English? Math? Why is it that none of them stick in my mind? I just don't remember them. I know that at some point I took those classes, but if it was that semester, if I had them on that day, I do not recall. It's hard to say if it even mattered what else I had that day. Chances are we probably spent the entire time talking about the twin towers. I doubt that any of our teachers would have stopped us that day. They probably would have joined in the conversation. How could you not? This was the Pearl Harbor moment of our generations. The television kept telling me that. The largest attack on American soil since Pearl Harbor. An estimated three thousand dead.

I recall the weeks that followed. Middle Eastern history and politics, which had been a small amount of the original history curricula was expanded to include Afghanistan. Mr. Franks brought in a student teacher with extensive knowledge of Afghanistan, at a time, I now recognise as being very fortunate, as everyone and their dog has since learned all about the various ethnic tribes of Afghanistan, their longstanding history of defeating foreign armies, and the importance of the illegal poppy trade.

14

To us, and to most people, it was all new. It only took a few years until I started skipping over the part of the newspaper where they were discussing Canada's future military options in Kandahar. I even gave up on trying to be pedantic and insisting that Afghanistan isn't actually part of the Middle East, but Central Asia. If the rest of the world was now saying that it is part of the Middle East, who am I to disagree? Maybe we could all insist that Canada is part of the European Union and it would become true, too.

I still have a hard time understanding how we got from A to B. I have struggled to understand how life continued onward from that fateful day. Was it always going to be so strange or did I just luck out into being born into a particular time and place?

"Is this the end, Sergey?"

"I don't know."

"I want to believe that it isn't."

"Why?"

Why did I want to believe that it wasn't the end? Perhaps it was a desire within myself to keep going, to keep moving forward with life. I was only sixteen years old. The world isn't allowed to end then. I wanted to have sex, for God's sake! I wanted to drink far too much alcohol. I wanted to be carried away in a cloud of marijuana smoke. The world couldn't end just yet, because I needed to live. It wouldn't be fair to me. Did September 11th change all that? Did this awful, tragic day actually alter the course of my life? Were there going to be milestones I would miss out on because of something that happed thousands of kilometers away?

There is a crushing blow to a person's soul when they realise that their own interests will always trump the interests of humanity at large. That each individual desire may be good for that person but it won't necessarily add to the march of progress at all. Every one of us has needs and wants and may go out of our way to get them. They won't add much to anyone else's life, but they feel good to us. It could be selfish, but why not be that way? It is easy enough to ignore at sixteen. It becomes an open wound upon genuine reflection later in life.

"They are not sure if this is going to affect the rugby tour."

"Why would it affect the rugby tour?"

"Because they say we might not be allowed to fly."

"That's ridiculous. Is the world going to stop all air travel?"

For weeks on end, it almost looked like they would. As a burgeoning athlete, my only concern was whether my high school team would get to travel to the United Kingdom in the spring. We had fundraised a lot of money and the alternative of taking a bus to California didn't really seem as appealing. California is a lovely place, but they are terrible at rugby.

I wanted to know why something that happened in New York, caused by Saudi Arabians, led to a war in Afghanistan. There would still be a strange link there, Mr. Franks' explanation notwithstanding. I wanted to know how all of this affected a rugby team from British Columbia traveling to Scotland. The links to why we couldn't travel were even more tenuous. I had heard that the world was a small place, but come on.

"What comes next?"

"Armageddon, I believe."

If it was the End Times, he would probably be right. Did we miss the Rapture? Was that still on?

"Sergey, you can't be serious."

"Cthulhu?"

"Now I know you aren't serious."

"Why, because I reference H.P. Lovecraft?"

"Yes."

"He could be a foreseer of things."

"I think he foresaw far too much opium."

"And the end of the world."

"How can you be so light about all this?"

"My family escaped the Soviet Union. I'm not worried about the world anymore."

Sergey's family had defected from the Soviet Union in one of the most exhilarating, if not comically mistimed, stories I had ever heard. It involved several flights, quick thinking, Prince Edward Island, Australia and South Korea. It also happened literally months before the Soviet Union collapsed anyways. Sergey's father, also called Sergey, never mentioned the daring escape, but his face always seemed to carry with it a hardness, the kind that one doesn't get without a few missteps in life or a bit of penance.

Just before the sixth grade, Sergey's family relocated again, this time in a far more conventional (and legal) move ending up in White Rock, where his parents ran some software company from their basement. Ever since then, Sergey and I had been best friends. Our unconventional thinking and light humour had kept us going. We would create characters and inside jokes. It was failing to connect on the one day when everyone needed their friends to just be friends.

"I'm serious, Sergey. I feel like the world is ending. Well, maybe not ending, but it is changing. Things have changed. What do we do now? Where do we go from this? Everything is messed up."

"Everything has always been messed up."

That may have been true. I don't know what sort of horrors Sergey had seen as a young boy in Vladivostok, but for a Canadian kid who had lived his whole life in the suburbs, it was a terrifying truth. I remember much later in life, out of some desire to connect with wherever I was, it might have been Palermo, reading Di Lampedusa and understanding that for things to stay the same, everything must change. On September 11th, for me, and my life, at least, nothing had changed while everything had changed.

I looked at Sergey and saw something for the first time. Beneath his normally cheerful exterior lay a deep melancholy. It was the real reason that we had been friends for all those years. He was just like me. We were part of a group of guys that just didn't seem to have what it took to be successful in high school, guys that would go on to do amazing things later in life, but were condemned to being known in those beige and green hallways as the Goof Troop.

"Yeah, I guess it has been."

We clung together for protection. It was easy to ignore all the jerks when we could just sit around in the hallway and make jokes. I never felt comfortable sitting in the cafeteria. There were cliques there and I was not a part of any of them. I wasn't a jock, even though I played sports. I wasn't a preppy, even though I liked and wore a lot of the same clothes (but would never define myself that way). I wasn't in French immersion, so I couldn't hang around with les gens français. I just didn't fit into any of their neatly defined groups. Neither did Sergey or any of the other guys in our troop. We were like the Island of Misfit Toys and that was quite alright. We'd create characters and stories out of thin air. We'd turn local newspaper columnists into minor celebrities (with or without pedophilic tendencies). We were able to just be, protected in our own little bubble.

We continued on like that until we graduated and then we all just drifted apart. Some of the guys stayed in close contact with each other, but more often than not, we just sort of drifted. I don't know if it happened that way or I imagine it happening that way now, but I tend to think that the bubble was popped on that day when Sergey told me the world was always messed up and I knew that he knew.

"Exactly. Now you can move forward with your life, just as you had previously planned."

Sergey didn't say that. I am certain of that. But it seems like the kind of thing that should be said at a moment like that. When the sky is falling, we need everyone to walk straight up to the Chicken Littles and say to them, "You know what, things will be fine", and walk away, leaving the worried bastards to contemplate the meaning of it all. If they were ready to go crazy over nothing, perhaps they'd be willing to live long, productive lives over something.

It's hard to see that when you are sixteen. It's hard to see anything beyond. I don't think I could sleep that night. I think I stayed awake far later than I ought to. It seemed like an obvious reason to lie wide awake, unsure of the world. It's around the same time that I must have developed insomnia. I don't know if there was a link or if I'm trying to create one long after the fact. By my rough calculations, at twenty-five I had been suffering insomnia for around ten years. Maybe it started with that night.

Stress and worrying are apparently causes of insomnia, along with poor diet, health, and substances such as caffeine or alcohol.

"What comes next?"

There was no one to answer that question. It was a void that couldn't be filled. Nothingness is a dark place, if it can even be thought of as a place, at all.

On Sundays we'd go to church.

"We pray for the tragic events of September 11th."

There's really not much that can be said about the good intentions of well-meaning people.

There's a ton that can be said about the evil intentions of awful, disgusting human beings, though. Especially the ones with cable television contracts.

Islam was examined from every angle, hoping to be "solved". They wanted to explain what could cause such a horrible loss of human life. They wanted to understand how something like this could come from a religion that called itself a way of peace.

It got ugly.

"Muslims don't want peace. They want to destroy everything about Western Civilization."
"Islam is about war. They only know the sword."

"Those terrorists would never have been Christians."

The hate popped up almost immediately. I don't recall if it was on the first day, but there were already connections being made between Mecca, Osama Bin Laden, the Taliban and average, law-abiding Muslims.

It made me uncomfortable. At the time, I identified as a Christian and was sickened by how willing people (of all beliefs) were to associate all believers of Islam with Islamic extremists.

The logic games were faulty.

"It is all in the Koran. They all believe this. Trust me."

No one wanted to say the same thing about the Bible. Oklahoma City had long been forgotten. We were being drawn into some Unholy War.

It had been maybe a year before that when I recall sitting in a prayer meeting that was asking for us to pray for the election of George W. Bush.

"He's a good Christian man. Exactly what the world needs."

It seemed like such a good idea. The problems with the world were that leaders weren't believers. Maybe it didn't dawn on our group that every American president, ever, had been a self-professing Christian. Maybe it was a cynical election requirement, but they all knew and loved Jesus. It hadn't changed a damned thing.

But I prayed for George Bush. I actually prayed that he would be elected. I almost feel like that was all my fault. If, of course, I still believed in the power of prayer.

It's not that I discount the possibility of God. It's certainly possible. It's just that I haven't seen convincing evidence that He particularly takes a hands-on approach with his Creation.

If He did, how can we explain one set of believers at war with another? Surely an activist God would intervene and tell them to behave or He was going to turn this world around, so help Him, er – God?

That's the only way I can still live with the knowledge that I prayed for Bush's election. I choose to believe that if God exists, He at least doesn't answer prayers. I choose to believe that I had nothing to do with the election. I am not American. I cannot vote in their elections. It was all the work of the electoral college and courts in Florida. It had nothing to do with a room full of praying students in Surrey.

But what if it did? What if all along we've been holding the power to move mountains? What if deep inside me there was some enormous potential to actually make a difference? What if deep inside each of us that was true?

If that's the case, then we've all been massive underachievers. I'm not sure that our memories will be kind to us. They will short circuit and fill in with all sorts of rubbish of missed opportunities and misspent energy. The nanobots that are supposed to repair damaged cells and ensure a steady flow of nutrients would go to waste. What good would come from that?

I think of all the time I spent dreaming of tomorrow. Tomorrow. That word seems so foreign to me now. It doesn't really exist anymore, does it? Time might move forward, I suppose, technically it will. But tomorrow will never come. It will just be a repeat of yesterday, won't it? It fills my heart with ache that I didn't seize enough days in my youth.

December 23, 2012

"You're breaking up with me?"

I didn't know what else to say to this unfortunate development.

"Yes."

"But Christmas is in two days."

"Would that make any difference?"

It wouldn't have made any difference. I knew that. Daphne had made up her mind and was leaving me. It was one of those things that just happens. The timing would never be great. There is never a good time to break up. There is a good time to start dating someone, though. It's called March 1st. If you begin dating someone then, it is at least a few weeks past Valentine's so that messiness doesn't get involved and then it is none of the really big holidays until the fall. Easter doesn't count. No one worries about bringing their date home for Easter dinner. It's not Thanksgiving. And then it is straight into the summer, which everyone knows is Primetime for Love™. It's often better to have a running head start, though, as that helps avoid the bubble bursting come September. But, in any case, there isn't a good time to break up with someone. Certainly not two days before Christmas.

I still had the receipt for her present. I guessed then that it could always be returned. There was going to be a big Boxing Week sale blow-out and I would return the necklace I had purchased and get something for myself. It's sad how little pleasure I got out of whatever it was that I replaced Daphne with. I can't even remember now. Was it a video game console? A stereo receiver? A digital video recorder? The mind blanks on those things over time.

Time. What a mindfuck time is. It can mess with you.

Daphne had it all: looks, taste, sophistication. I swear she was the one for me. The one that got away. If there had been a movie about our life together, I would have been the lovable loser played by John Cusack and Daphne would have been the "way out of his league, I can't believe they are trying to sell us this garbage" Scarlett Johansson. We've all seen that type of movie a thousand times, but it becomes far more unbelievable when it happens in real life. Most of the time, I've found myself on the outside complaining about gorgeous women that end up with awful men. Sitting down on Marine Drive in White Rock on a summer day provides an amazing array of examples. There were plenty of ersatz men wearing long shorts and tank tops walking around with their hands on the waist of women far too good looking for them to be natural. Were those men incredibly wealthy? Were those woman incredibly stupid? Could it be that somehow each of those ridiculous looking displays of masculinity actually possessed a charming and enchanting personality that would win over even the most particular of beauties? I had my doubts about that, but then again, I always had suspicions that people might have been whispering similar things about how I had managed to capture a ten like Daphne.

We sat in that tiny booth in a basement sushi restaurant in Yaletown and I tried my best to figure out what had just happened. Not how I had ended up with Daphne. That was a mystery that I can't quite recall. No, I had come to terms with the unbelievable good fortune I had. It was not about how that had began that confused me. It was the opposite. Daphne had just ended things between us. She was making a final statement about where our relationship was at. All the whispering about us would no longer be about how I managed to stay with her, but how I had even managed to be with her at all. It would grow in size and the speculation would become legendary. It would also serve notice to the jackals that liked to pounce that Daphne was now available and that I was out of the picture. It had become clear that we were not to be together anymore. I remember that moment like it was yesterday. I had just finished a piece of my spicy tuna, but hadn't quite gotten to my spider roll.

"I think we are just at different places in our lives."

She tried to make a compelling case, but the contrarian in me just wanted to scream out that it was impossible for us to be at two different places when we were sharing the same booth. I wanted to scream "No! No! No! You're wrong!", but that isn't the sort of thing that wins a woman's heart back, is it? It's hard to fight these things when you know that you hold no advantage whatsoever. She had always been out of my league and only now she had just realised it. All this time I had been playing with house money, I couldn't complain about my luck.

"What do you mean?"

Daphne had a sigh that was one part patience and two parts exasperation. If you didn't know her you'd have thought it was all exasperation. If you knew me, you'd be impressed with her ability to at least throw in the one part patience.

"I'm not entirely convinced that you know what you want out of life."

I was entirely convinced that she was right. It was a correct assessment of who I was and where I was at in life (aside from a Yaletown sushi bar). I was just amazed it took her three years to figure it out. Daphne was an extremely intelligent woman, a fact that became harder to believe the more that I looked back on it in retrospect. How intelligent could she have been if she was too obtuse to realise that I had no idea what I wanted out of my life. It had taken her three years to come to that conclusion. I may have even spared her the time when I probably announced as much of a fact on our first date. Maybe she had realised then and thought she could change me. Everyone wanted to change everyone back then. That was the success in self-help books. There were large international markets out there that were making fortunes on the premise. Maybe she was filled with confidence that I would be a really easy project, a simple fixer-upper. Daphne must have looked at me in the same way that a contractor looked at a brick Georgian townhouse with "good bones".

"Is that a deal breaker?"

"Yes! Please, I thought I made that clear enough. I don't think this can go on much longer."

I still hadn't touched my spider roll. It just sat there on the plate next to the half-empty tray of soya sauce mixed with flecks of wasabe. I was hoping that our relationship could last long enough for me to finish eating.

"I thought you were just looking for a bit of fun."

I knew better than to say that. The type of women that were looking for a bit of fun would have long grown bored with me. I enjoyed reading the works of Hunter S. Thompson, but I had no desire to go on a drug-filled siege of Las Vegas. I had no problem setting an alarm clock and punching in for a day's work and then returning to home to watch television curled up next to my partner. I had no idea what house music was. I thought that might just be whatever you played in your home. It was very similar to what I would choose for car music.

"I was, at first. But, well, we've been together for a while now. More than a few years. For God's sake, we're both twenty-seven and not getting any younger."

I looked at Daphne and for the first time I really realised how far she was out of my league. It was one of those facts that I probably had known for so long that it stopped being real and I could just begin to ignore and discount it at will. Exactly the sort of taking someone for granted behaviour that often leads to break-ups. Daphne really was too gorgeous for me. Her perfect features were only accented by her sour mood. When she was serious it made her look like a model. She had that kind of model pout. Not a supermodel, per se, but she would not have been out of place in a department store catalogue.

There was nothing I liked more in the world than seeing her walk around in my apartment in nothing but a t-shirt and panties. It really got me going. Perhaps it was a school boy fantasy realised, but the look of a woman partially clothed caused blood to rush to the extremities.

I had already suspected as much, but hearing her say our respective ages made me see that she was a twenty-seven year old woman in mint condition and I was the twenty-seven year old man that could be sold by a used car salesman as "well-loved".

Even calling me a twenty-seven year old man was being generous. My birth certificate said I was that old, but my behaviour certainly must have skewed me younger. I still enjoyed reading comic books. I called them graphic novels, but I don't think Daphne particularly cared for the semantics.

"What would it take?"

My face pleaded for attention. It was a last, desperate grasp at my crumbling life. My crumbling life: a brick Georgian townhouse with "good bones" built on an eroding cliff of inertia.

"I'm sorry?"

"What would it take to keep us together?"

I wanted a simple answer. I wanted her to tell me that it was all part of a three-step program to manhood. Just a few easy steps on the way to spending my life in bliss with a beautiful woman forever. I'd even read the guidebook if Daphne placed it in my hands. I'd have to probably take a weekend course, but we could work it around the various sports I usually watched (soccer and rugby in the morning and hockey at night).

"You're a creature of habit. You are who you are and it is a wonderful person, but it's not enough for me anymore. I'm sorry."

She stood up, grabbed her coat, scarf and mitts and walked away from the table. I watched her stand by the restaurant door as she prepared to enter the cold, wet air. It might have been around five degrees outside. I ate my spider roll.

It was a shock to go home. Daphne and I had never actually moved in together, but had somehow managed to create enough of our presence at each other's apartments that it became eerily apparent how much was missing of her at mine. I looked around and ostensibly the flat hadn't changed noticeably to the naked eye. I still had four walls and a floor. The paint hadn't changed colours. The pictures that I had framed still hung there. The fern that I had foolishly purchased was dying in the corner. Everything was the same. It was just little things that had disappeared.

Opening up the kitchen cupboard to pour myself a glass of water I saw the cheap dollar store mug that Daphne had picked out for me on a date early in our relationship (third? sixth?). It was decorated with a repetitive print pattern of dolphins. I don't know why she picked that one out for me. I don't think it symbolises anything significant or anything. I think she just liked dolphins. Who didn't? They were among the most intelligent creatures on earth, and if Douglas Adams is to be believed, far superior to even humans. I miss them. On the same date, I had picked out a mug for Daphne that had a crocodile on it. I don't think that I meant for it to be symbolic either, but I was far clumsier in those sort of things. Perhaps my subconscious made a connection. It was a cool looking mug in any case, with the crocodile a bright neon green colour. We returned to my apartment that night and watched a stack of movies (Kill Bill parts 1&2, the Wedding Singer, and 10 Things I Hate About You – one of these was Daphne's choice), and we drank orange pop out of those mugs.

I couldn't find the crocodile mug in the cupboard. Had it migrated to Daphne's place a while before? Perhaps holding a transient cup of coffee, even though there was no lid. Did she pack it up with her things when she knew she was done with me? Did that happen? Did she come through the apartment when I wasn't home and gather every last morsel of our connection? I don't recall a giant box by the door marked "death". Could the mug have disappeared in a completely unrelated manner, the way that socks innocuously disappear?

Daphne hated my socks. Maybe hate is a stretch, but she always had to comment about my socks. When I was lounging about barefoot, she'd ask why I wasn't wearing any socks.

"Um, because I like being barefoot?"

When I'd wear socks, they'd always be the wrong socks. I'd wear ankle socks with pants, which was a big no-no, or the wrong colour socks to match my shoes or belt or hat or whatever garment socks are meant to match. Is it umbrella? It must be umbrella. I ought to have worn more black socks to match my umbrella.

The crocodile mug was gone. So was the shower organizer. It's amazing what things a woman will choose to take when a relationship is over. I missed the clearing out box. I didn't get a chance to stop her. She could have left the shower organizer. There is no way that could have been too painful to leave behind. Where was I supposed to put my shampoo and shower gel? On the side of the tub? In those corners that get inexplicably more dirty than the rest of the bath? It had been years since I had lived so uncouthly. I might have taken the break-up better if Daphne had at least left me the shower organizer. A well managed assortment of bathroom accoutrements is probably good for the reduction of stress, or something like that. If cleanliness was next to Godliness, tidiness might have been up there, too.

At the time, I tried to think of the things that I needed to collect from Daphne's apartment. I wanted her to feel the same emptiness I felt. I wanted to go in and rip something permanent right out from the relationship walls of her metaphorical apartment. I wanted her to feel hurt. I wanted her to miss the equivalent of a crocodile mug or a shower organizer. I wanted her to have physical reminders in every room that I was no longer a part of her life. For the life of me, I couldn't come up with anything that she would miss.

In three years of time-sharing (the best description of our living arrangements), I don't think I ever actually made much of a permanent physical impression on Daphne's apartment. I left the occasional drink on the coffee table without a coaster that left watermarks, sure, but Daph was quick enough to wipe those up before they left irreversible, irrevocable damage. There was nothing permanent like that. Nothing I could rest my mind in knowing that she would always have to be reminded of me. I felt like sneaking into her apartment and just creating some water rings. I wanted her to have to stare at it every time she put her drink down, even if it meant her putting her drink down on a coaster that hid the water rings from the naked eye. She would know, that underneath lay a permanent reminder of me. I would never leave her. I would never leave her, until she replaces her living room furniture.

She obviously created space in the fridge for the things that I liked. There would be a four pack of Guinness cans every now and then. But Daphne hated Guinness. She wouldn't miss that being in her fridge. She wouldn't miss the near tragedies every time it got near the coffee table, either. That wasn't enough to make her regret leaving me. It wasn't enough for her to miss me if she never liked it. It would never be in her fridge again. I couldn't even remember the last time it was, in any case. It had been a while. October? August? It hadn't even been enough of a routine that I missed it being in her fridge when we were together. Hell, I couldn't recall the last time I had it in my own fridge.

My clothes didn't take up much space. I had been given half a drawer a long time ago and had never felt the need to ask for additional space. It's just not the sort of thing that I felt the need to ask for. I always managed to have plenty of clothes, and my apartment wasn't really all that far away, just a hop on a bus or the train. Close enough that I never really had to worry about a change. We weren't one of those couples that holed ourselves up over an entire weekend and didn't see daylight, anyways. Daphne would never allow that. She was active, which probably explained how she maintained her great looks. That forced me to be active, too. I took up running. I'd run around False Creek, or the Seawall. I usually showered at my own apartment, where I had an entire dresser filled with my own clothes. It was probably never even discussed that if I had more space at Daphne's I would be able to return from my run, shower and change there without any issue. With half a drawer, though, I needed to keep just the bare essentials. There were a pair of jeans, some t-shirts, underwear, socks and one pair of pyjama bottoms. Half a drawer in Daphne's wardrobe wouldn't even account for her pyjamas. Is that all the space that I took up? Could I be replaced by a few sets of pyjamas?

Daphne had always mentioned that my best feature was keeping her warm at night. The thought that my single greatest contribution to our relationship could be replaced by flannel and a block heater never occurred to me until long after.

"Mmm, thanks doll. You're the best teddy bear ever."

Despite what everyone says, a heart can be broken over and over again. It is the most fragile thing, like fine glasswork. It is beautiful and in the right possession can be put on display for all to admire. It sits there and provides a focal point. Something to love and cherish until it falls from that top shelf. The tiny fragments get pieced together, like a vase with super glue, and begin life anew, though never quite fixed. It gets placed back on the shelf and from the right angles is still quite beautiful, but never the same. It might topple over again. The glue comes out once more. Back on the shelf. Topple. Glue. Shelf.

I don't remember anything from that Christmas. I think I called my sister Ashley that night that Daphne had left me and told her not to expect us for dinner on Christmas Day. Ashley told Mom and Dad, who both tried to call me, but I chose to let those calls go to voicemail. I appreciated their love and affection, but it was too close, too similar to what I had just lost. It's like giving a child a new puppy after their old dog was put to sleep. It is nice, but it's not the same, and will never be.

"We're just worried about you."

"We just want you to know that we love you."

"Are you okay?"

"Call us back, please."

"I'm making stuffing just the way you like it."

"Listen, it's not to pressure you or anything, but I think it might be nice if you made the effort of spending Christmas with your family. We love you and think that it might do you some good to feel that. Oh no, I didn't mean to say that you weren't feeling loved. I'm sorry, dear. I didn't mean that. Of course you are loved."

The next time I saw Daphne was a few days after Christmas. It wasn't quite New Year's Eve then. I knew that much. I had a post-it note on my fridge reminding me to call the restaurant where we had reservations and to cancel. I still hadn't done that. I wasn't looking forward to the cancellation fee that the restaurant charged on New Year's. Maybe I was hoping that Daphne would come back. Maybe I was hoping I could give the reservation to some friends. Maybe I would go for dinner alone. If I cancelled my credit card was going to get charged anyways, I might as well get a nice meal out of it, even if I am alone on supposedly one of the most romantic evenings of the year.

Daphne had wanted to clear the air and drop off my things from her apartment. She felt it would be best if we met in a neutral location, so I chose a coffee shop on Georgia. It was a foolish decision as the place was packed with people in the midst of their Boxing Week shopping, popping in for a latte. I don't know if I had exchanged Daphne's necklace for the game console or receiver or recorder or whatever it was yet. Whatever it was, I remember it being significantly reduced on sale.

"How are you doing?"

"Fine."

She looked at me with her big hazel eyes that sparkled with the light of Saturn's rings and smiled a pitiful smile. She really was a god coming down from the clouds to grace me with her presence. How did she ever manage to spend all those years with a mere mortal, such as I?

"I'm really sorry. I know this is harsh, but for us both to grow as individuals, it's best that we move on."

The box filled with all the relics of our broken relationship looked mockingly small sat atop the coffee shop table, with plenty of space for Daphne's cappuccino and my eggnog latte. I was expecting the box to be much larger, as if time and stuff were a linear regression.

"This eggnog latte sure is good."

"Don't be like that."

"Be like what?"

"That. Don't be all guarded and defensive."

It was truly hard to express myself when I didn't know exactly what to say or do. I was the one who was dumped. I didn't think that I needed to explain myself or my behaviour.

"I was commenting on my eggnog latte."

"Exactly! That's what's wrong with you. You don't want to talk about what is wrong with you or us or anything. You'd be happy to spend the rest of your life drinking that eggnog latte."

She was wrong. I would have spent hours, days even, talking about what was wrong with me or her and us together. I would have done that if it meant that we could be together. I thought I had tried to do that at the sushi restaurant just a few days before. A week after a break-up isn't the time to start discussing what could have gone better. People who are dumped aren't looking for a post-mortem or a list of things to work on for the next person. I wanted to know what I could actively do then to save my relationship and it had been made abundantly clear up to that point that the answer was nothing. There was nothing I could do. Discussion wasn't going to solve anything.

"I would, but it is a limited edition thing. Seasonal, actually. They only carry it around the holidays."

Daphne looked at me with exhaustion. Every ounce of her wanted to tell me off, but she restrained. I think that a part of her realised that I had gone into my shell because that is what a near-defenceless creature does.

"I am sorry, you know. You've been a great boyfriend. You have. We've had fun. I want you to know that. I just, well, I just don't know how much I want you to be my husband or the father of my children. You're just always going to be that guy who would rather drink an eggnog latte."

She seemed fixated on my choice of beverage. I wanted to understand what that meant. I wanted to know what the significance of my choosing an eggnog latte was. If we had broken up at Thanksgiving would she have been berating my choice of a pumpkin spice latte?

"I don't know what that means."
"For God's sake!"

Daphne jumped out of her seat and in a frantic endeavour tried to pull her coat on. It would be cruel to say that she made a fool out of herself that afternoon, but she did. I may have been a man who was content to drink an eggnog latte, but when I finished, I calmly put on my charcoal pea coat and left the café with my dignity. Also a tiny box of the shattered remains of my relationship.

It's funny, I guess, how up until you're forced to carry the actual sum total of three years with a woman that you think it ought to weigh more, or take up more space, or actually be filled with meaning.

When I got home, I put the Break-Up Box on my couch and begin rifling through it. To my astonishment, Daphne had kept some keepsakes for herself. Nowhere in the box were any love letters or cards or any other paper memorabilia, which in my younger days had been standard procedure to return. It was nice to think that I had at least spent the past three years with a sentimental woman. Or at the very, very least, a considerate woman who didn't need to show me the recycling bin where she had discarded my affections.

Instead, I was left with a ponderous collection of hygiene essentials (toothbrush, toothpaste, floss, deodorant, shower gel, and lens cleaner), out-of-rotation clothing, and movies I had probably never watched at Daphne's or my apartment. Were they even mine? There is no way I had ever owned The Transporter 2, was there? It's not that I didn't mind Jason Statham movies, it was just that, well, to be honest, I can't recall why I found it so shocking that The Transporter 2 was in the box, it just was.

That was the sum total of three years of my peak adult life. Quite literally, as I had been in a relationship from when I was twenty-four until I was twenty-seven. I could see Daphne's point about wanting to move on. Who could have wanted to waste their prime on me? There was a very small sliver of time left before the biological clock started ticking much more rapidly and certain things become more important.

That might have been the strangest realisation of my (relatively) young life, to agree with the assessment of The One Who Got Away. It brought a strange relief and a pressure at the same time. I had been someone's wasted years. How could I be that way? How was it possible to just drift from place to place for years at a time, letting inertia carry me? How could I be an empty void that sucked in everything and everyone around him?

I could understand a ten like Daphne wanting more than that. I could understand that she needed to find a real man, a partner, someone who would be everything she needed. Someone who would contribute, not take. I could see her living in some cul-de-sac with two and a half kids, a golden retriever and an SUV. I could see that and could feel that as much as I might have disparaged that thought before, it was exactly what I wanted.

June 16, 2006

I stood in nervous anticipation. There was a bit of sweat building up underneath my armpits and just below the solar plexus. I hoped that it wasn't going to show. I was always unsure whether the colour of shirt I chose highlighted sweat spots. It wasn't that I was excessively sweaty, it was just that standing around in the summer sun didn't do any favours. Being nervous obviously wasn't helping me then, either.

I don't know what it was about her, but Carrie made my knees weak. They got all wobbly and I turned to mush. It was a surprise that I was able to stand upright at all. Carrie had that effect on me. There was a strong defiance in her presence that said to the world that she existed and that no protestations from the universe were going to deny it. She was bold, perhaps even brash. She was stubborn and carried herself through life that way, as if allowing even a hint of weakness would have the universe implode around her. It wasn't about letting the universe come to her. She would go out into it herself. Carrie didn't wait for those opportunities to arise, she created them. She would leave her mark out there. Eventually she would leave her mark with me.

In contrast, I don't think that I was ever as notable. I somehow think that the universe could have erased me from everyone's memory a long time ago. That perhaps I was such a small part of anyone's memory that if every word of someone's life was written in a long, possibly billion page long scroll, my name might appear once or twice. Small enough to disappear without notice. Small enough to be mistaken for a typo. In the long intertwined histories of every person I've ever met, would their combined interactions with me sum up to something worthwhile. Did I add anything to this universe? Would I be missed if my name was stricken from all records? Maybe it has been.

I stood out on the sidewalk with nothing to do to keep myself occupied. I just stood there dumbly. I probably fidgeted a little bit. I don't know if I ever actually twiddled my thumbs, but that would have been the most natural way for me to fidget with nothing to keep me busy. If we had gone on a first date five years later, I'd have waited with my face buried in a smartphone, sifting through emails, reading news articles or searching for a song to listen to. Smartphones were such great inventions, they fit perfectly into the hands, built to respond to twiddling thumbs. Built to fill the empty voids that took up so much of our lives in between the supposed milestones. But the universe didn't deliver me to Carrie five years later. Or Carrie didn't reach out into the universe and deliver herself to me five years later. I don't want to dwell on the ontology of it all, too much anyways, the point was about timing.

I can't remember who said it, whether it was someone famous or whether it was a friend or family member, but at some point in my life I do remember being instilled with the thought that we should be thankful for the experiences that we have, when we have them, because they were meant to happen when they did. The same can be said for the people that come in and out of our lives. Each one of them is supposed to apparently play a role in helping define who we are.

I don't think I realised it then, but Carrie would have a profound impact on my life for years to come long after she had gone. I would still think of her in whatever way you could describe thinking about an ex without it seeming strange or creepy. I didn't really pine over her, but there were moments where I would miss the little things in life that she brought. I think we are allowed to miss people like that. It doesn't necessarily mean that we wanted them back or that we wanted to dwell in the past. It is just that there are certain things or moments that will carry with you forever. But that's skipping ahead more than a bit.

Before our first date, I had been flirtatious with Carrie for quite a while. She was cute, I was human – it was bound to happen. It's hard to avoid being drawn towards such a radiant person. I was certainly drawn, but I didn't necessarily make it clear from the start. Maybe it was my slow moving ways, or maybe it was out of fear of her strong presence, but it took me months to approach her for a date. I don't know what she thought of me before, but I could tell from the way she walked up to me on that first date and wrapped her arms around me warmly that there was a connection.

"Hi."

A smile went across her broad face and I looked at her with more than a little bit of interest. I told a lie just now. Not that she didn't fill me with interest – she did. No, I said I worked up the courage to approach Carrie for a date – I didn't. In fact, I had meant to just see if she wanted to hang out casually. I didn't know before whether it was a date or just two friends hanging out. The warmth of the hug told me it was a date. I don't know how I could have mistaken it for anything but a date. I don't know how she would have read my intentions as anything but a young man attracted to her declaring his intentions. Were there lots of young male/female couples who hung out without the intention of hooking up? Did I imagine that as a concept? It has been so long that I don't trust my memory sometimes. It would have been a wonderful thing to know that anytime a female wanted to hang out with me it was because she found me sexually desirable. That would have cleared up so much confusion over the years. It is far too late now, but in any future lives I might get to live, it would be an asset to know.

We sat across from each other and chatted harmlessly. It was one of those conversations that seemed standard for a first date. Questions were asked about favourite activities, movies, and music – that sort of thing. It was a bit like a job interview, as far as I remember. I'd have a rote list of things that I'd have to work into the conversation. These were things that I needed to include to demonstrate my ability for the job. If prospective girlfriends required cover letters, I might have known what to include back then. In any case, it would have been quite hard to maintain a professional interview with someone as attractive as Carrie.

She was dressed in a tight t-shirt and a skirt that showed off her bronzed legs nicely. It was still early in the summer, and despite it still being what we liked to call on the coast "Juneuary", Carrie looked like she had already had a full year's amount of sun.

Maybe that is how I remember her. Maybe that is how I remember that meeting. Perhaps I am idealising everything. Did every detail seem so wonderful? Was her hug really as warm as I recall or was it just the sweat below my solar plexus? Did she really have such golden legs? I remember how pale she looked in the winter. Was that year-round or did she gain a tan in the summer? Would she have been tanned in June, in any case?

When everything has been bleak and grey, it doesn't take too much of a trickle of light to radiate everywhere. My mind can sometimes add details that I don't really remember being there. Had I missed them before, but they had always rested there in my subconscious? Did I rediscover new things that had always been there every new time that I recalled a memory? Or did I just start fabricating things that never were? I could be wrong. It's been known to happen before.

I was twenty-one then and heading into my last year of university in the fall and Carrie entered my life like a bulldozer. It's startling to think of how weak my entire life's foundation had been up until then. A bulldozer may not have been necessary. A strong wind would have done the trick. It would come as no surprise to know which of the three little pigs I most resembled.

"You're a goof."

I don't know what I did exactly to warrant that comment. Was I playful? Sure. I can be playful. It wouldn't have been out of character. I am not positive that I was being playful, but the knowledge that I could be at times is enough to justify considering that as a possibility. Was I awkward? Yes. Certainly, I must have been. I didn't know any other way. I had been unapologetically awkward my entire life, before and after Carrie. But what was it in particular that garnered her attention, that I do not know.

"Thanks?"

"Ha, too funny."

Humans have this uncanny ability to be amused by the slightest of things when sexual desire – and crucially, the potential for sexual satisfaction – is at play. We will go far out and away from anything that might be considered "normal" or "natural" behaviour if we thought that it might lead to intercourse. It is the culmination of numerous generations of ancestors faking interest in things for hours on end in exchange for a few minutes of pleasure. We've got all sorts of genetic abilities passed down over millennia of mating. Somehow, I still managed to be a timid and lame pursuer of the fairer sex.

"I like how you just put your hand on my knee."

"Um, you're welcome?"

"It was such an elementary school move."

I had no idea what kind of elementary Carrie went to, but it must have been filled with experiences that outdid any of mine. I don't recall any opportunities where a girl would let me touch her. I was still trying to get my head past how similar the concepts of cooties and STDs were.

"Oh."

"Don't worry, it was reciprocated – clearly. I just thought it was funny how you made that move."

Funny? This was life and death stuff to me and a game to Carrie. Doesn't she know that our species must continue! We must recreate! We wore condoms for practice, to make sure that we were doing it right. Whenever humans finally got around to having children, I wanted to believe it was because they were well-practiced and ready to bring life into the world. I clearly just wasn't anywhere near ready for that sort of responsibility. I wanted to work my way towards that human obligation. I did, I really did want that. It would require a lot of practice, but I was willing to serve my time.

How badly I wanted Carrie to find me attractive, how I craved that. It was a deep, dark longing that would have validated my entire existence. Who I was, the history I had created, whatever my name was written down as, all of that no longer mattered. That was not funny at all. The way that she would come in and bulldoze my life, which was an already weak foundation, twisting and crumbling to her every need and whim, that was not funny either. But how could I have known that? How could I have seen that by submitting myself in every way to a more powerful force would leave me open and vulnerable to destruction? How could I have seen that coming? What sort of powers of foresight could I have been equipped with? It is all well and good to look back with hindsight for all eternity, but there is nothing I can do now to change the way she pulverised me into the smallest fragments of dust.

The place where we finally broke up one year later was sort of funny. It was the same place as our first date. That is funny. I can see the ironic humour in that now. Symmetry is funny.

At the time, way back then, I didn't know any of that. I couldn't have seen that Carrie was a woman built with all that force. There was nothing inside me that was able to detect danger and protect accordingly. All of my deepest fears were based around the horrible premise that I might die alone. I would have done anything to avoid that. I didn't think that it would be far more painful to die alone and heartbroken. Was it Tennyson who said it was better to have loved and lost than never have loved at all? He was an idiot. Ignorance would have been bliss. I could have lived my life without any heartache and died alone as some peaceful hermit. Instead I am doomed to rest my remaining days with the images of everything I had lost replaying over and over again. I couldn't have predicted that way back then. I just saw this golden girl with the broad face who thought I was cute.

Looking back, with retrospective eyes, people try to draw conclusions about the time wasted in a relationship and whatever sort of positive lessons could be learned. They want to add meaning. They want to think that it wasn't all wasted. They all just want to think that every decision they've made can be justified in the cosmic abacus. They dwell on crystallising moments, the ones that seem to define and sum up everything about the relationship between those two people. There are fights. There are tear-filled phone calls. There are steamy acts of public sex.

Jericho Park was the victim of several trysts between Carrie and I. We'd make love in the back seat of a car in the parking lot or lie on the sand and perform manual stimulation on each other. The electric charge and tension that came from the possibility of getting caught added to the excitement. I wasn't just having sex with a beautiful girl, but someone powerful, someone with authority might catch us. The sexuality of our relationship, the intimacy that kept us close together, came from the secrecy involved. Carrie and I both lived at home with our parents, who, in their own ways, greatly disapproved of pre-marital sex. We weren't just growing together as a couple, drawn by pheromones, but it was protest. These were acts of defiance against individuals – against a society – that were trying to keep us apart. Every time we came together we were stoking the revolution. To be twenty and fighting a war with your lips is a magical thing.

Years later, when I was living in Yaletown, I'd sometimes head across the Burrard Street bridge and run out past Jericho without any real intentions. My legs would pump up and down and I'd propel forward. My lower back would start to ache. I'd wipe my brow and keep pushing on. I wouldn't be anywhere near finished until the goal was achieved. I wasn't a quitter. I'd reach Spanish Bank and just stand hunched over my knees in sweaty exhaustion and waves of old memories would cross over me.

Would it ever be enough? Would I ever be enough? I wondered those things silently as I sought to please Carrie in a way that I had never pleased anyone before. I was young and insecure. I had been a relative latecomer to the sexual revolution. I needed to make up for lost time. There were plenty of battles left to fight. I just wanted her to know that I cared and that I was giving it my everything.

Carrie took everything that I would give, in a spiritual and emotional sense, anyways. I was drawn into her star. She placed herself into the universe, remember. She defined the terms of orbit. It wasn't up for me to decide the patterns of rotation or whether or not I would be eclipsed. I would be. That is just the way things went, I suppose. Our entire time together was characterised by my effort to be anything she wanted me to be. I seemed to have no problem with that, then. I was willing to devote myself to the star and let her warmth trickle outwards to me. It was about me trying to be the partner she thought she needed. Asymmetric, I suppose. An unequal partner, if that can be called a partner at all. I catered to her every need. I even literally catered for her, spending one evening making hors d'oeuvres for her friends. I made myself available to her.

At least I thought I did. Looking back, I can see that by abandoning who I was, I was doing a disservice to both Carrie and myself. Who would want to love a sycophant? Only tyrants, I suppose. Though she was strong-willed, Carrie was no tyrant.

"You can put your hand on my leg anytime."
"Oh, that's good."

I beamed. What a generous benefactor. I enjoyed it when the sun poured out onto the face of the earth. I thought that was all that was needed for flowers to grow and for birds to sing.

"So, what music do you like?"

Music. Oh, for the love of music. If there is one area where I can thank Carrie all these years later it is that she, more than any other ex-girlfriend, contributed positively to my love and knowledge of music.

While I had always enjoyed melodic and melancholic music, in theory, at least, I didn't have much broad knowledge of or experience with it. Carrie introduced me to Bright Eyes and Belle & Sebastian, to which I'll always be indebted to her.

On weekends when her parents were out of town, we'd lie in bed and Conor Oberst's voice would tremor beside us. Between the orange bed sheets and us lay love of a certain time. It had an expiry date, if only because Carrie's father, a stern man, if there ever was one, would return eventually. If someone were to ask you what it means to be young, I'd hope that you'd paint a similar picture to us in that orange bed. There would be nothing sweeter for a young man than to wake beside a beautiful creature in his arms.

Breakfast would be something simple and easy, probably cereal, but occasionally more elaborate than that. French toast, perhaps, with a glass of orange juice, an orange wholly unlike the colour of the sheets, but fully orange in its own right. Carrie wouldn't usually wish to waste too much time with breakfast. There was a limit to how much time we would have together and small details like sleep or food could drift away in favour of longer sessions of love-making.

I don't know if I knew on that first date that it would all unfold like that. I'd like to think that I could tell from that first warm hug. There might have been some metaphysical transference that passed between us. A telekinetic connection that held some foresight.

It certainly didn't foresee the entire future. My, what screw-ups we all are.

We booked a hotel in Seattle. Carrie wanted to take me to see the Mariners as a gift. Despite their stubborn unwillingness to be competitive, I had been a fan of the Seattle Mariners since I was a young boy. They were the closest team geographically, and though the Toronto Blue Jays and the eventually defunct Montreal Expos tried to rally support from Canadians of all regions, it was still hard to cheer for a team so far away. It was hard to imagine a team three time zones away being my local team.

When we crossed the border, it was early in the season, but late in our relationship. The Mariners won, oddly enough. I can't remember the score, but I do remember Ichiro hitting a home run. It was amazing to see the M's win. It had been years since I had seen it in person. Almost without fail every road trip I took with Dad and Ashley resulted in a Mariners loss. I guess Carrie was my good luck charm or something that day. We returned to the room and Carrie lay down to rest for a bit. Fair enough, I thought. We had both drank a few too many beers and absorbed quite a lot of sun. I made sure she had a big glass of water before she went to nap. It was best to avoid sunstroke or just plain dehydration.

I don't know what came over me, but I thought I'd do something romantic and draw a bubble bath for us both. It seemed like a really good idea. It seemed like the sort of thing that a good boyfriend would do when on vacation with the love of his life. She never joined me.

I'm not sure if there is a sadder image than a man having a romantic bubble bath for one.

"Sorry, I wasn't feeling well."
"That's okay."
"Are you mad at me?"
"No."

I was. I don't even know if I had a right to be mad, but I was. I know now that she probably was feeling awful because of the beer and the sun, but we were on vacation. It was supposed to be a great weekend in Seattle without any concerns or worries. A chance to spend some quality time together. Did I expect too much? Did I not understand what a woman wants from a romantic getaway? It seemed like even when I was trying my hardest it was always in the wrong direction or it wasn't done right. Was I set up to lose her?

We had sex against the window of the hotel suite at Carrie's suggestion.

"That was great."

"Yeah."

So many signs in the rear-view mirror can provide a better glimpse at where we've been than our current location.

June 15, 2011

I waited for Daphne by the door. I didn't want to make a fuss, but I was feeling that we were running late. Didn't she understand that this was supposed to be a huge day? I was one victory away from watching my boyhood team win their first Stanley Cup.

"They might lose."

Daphne always had a way of putting things in perspective. It was one of her best assets. It didn't always resonate with others because of her particular delivery. It was both cheery and gloomy at the same time. I found it very interesting that there was almost no contradiction in the way that she was able to communicate those positions. Mom described her as a "complex" girl. Ashley avoided trying to describe any girls that I dated.

"Are you ready, Daph? We really should be making a move."

I was beginning to regret spending the night at Daphne's apartment. It was a pleasant enough night, but geographically, it meant that we were that much further away from the viewing party than if we had stayed at my place.

"You sure you don't just want to watch it on T.V.?"

My face betrayed homicidal thoughts.

"Fine. We'll go to this stupid viewing party and stand like sardines for hours on end. I hope you are happy."
"You know I am."

She wouldn't let me suffer the agony of watching the Canucks hoist the Cup without some random stranger to high-five. He would be drunk and sweaty and I'd throw my hand up to meet his and we'd smile stupid grins. We would be so happy that we would remember that moment forever, that day when we gave a high-five to a stranger and it was totally cool. There was no shame in giving a high-five when sports championships were involved. It wasn't like that time that they gave out free doughnuts. That wasn't high-five worthy, in retrospect. Though it didn't stop us from trying to make it so. No, if the Vancouver Canucks were to hoist the Stanley Cup, there would be nothing unacceptable about a high-five from a stranger in the streets. Daphne certainly wasn't going to give me a high-five. She barely gave me hand jobs any more.

We boarded the Canada Line and already I could see that Daphne was uncomfortable. Her body firmed up and her posture became more closed. She put her arms across her chest and frowned. Daphne made eye contact with me and then nudged her head towards the direction of some drunken louts sprawled over the floor. They had spilled beer beside them and half-full cans in their hands.

"B-b-b-b-ston sucks."

"Ugh, yep. Tha's right. It sure is."

Daphne looked at me and rolled her eyes. It would have bothered me normally, because I knew she found a complex way to make the rolling of eyes not just be about the drunken louts, but also about the value judgment of their statement. It was as if she was in disagreement that the Bruins sucked. I wanted her to agree with that statement. I needed her to validate my choice of team. We had to be in this together. She didn't have to agree with the awful way that the drunkard said it, but at the heart, she had to agree. I would have been upset, but Daphne had been a good sport and had joined in the festivities all season. I think almost every Saturday night had begun with her letting me watch the game. We'd then watch a movie or go out for drinks. Sometimes it would be something as simple as going for a walk. Life was good with Daphne.

We enjoyed a blissful state of affairs in those days. I'd spend half my nights at her apartment and she would spend half her nights at mine. It had rarely happened where we wouldn't spend the night together. A couple times when I was sick, she would come and take care of me in the evening, but then head home. I didn't mind that, as she clearly didn't want to miss work due to my awful germs. She always gave me enough cold medicine to knock me out for the night. Once, I went out with the boys and got too drunk to make it to either of our places. I think I spent the night on the floor next to a couch. When I woke up I found three voicemails and fifteen text messages from Daphne, such were the unusual circumstances of that night. She really did care and miss me. Oddly enough, whenever Daphne went out drinking and dancing with her girlfriends, she would always return home to me, often with a renewed sexual vigour. I never got the chance to thank the gay men she danced with.

That's not just me adding a layer of insecurity into my memories. I don't just remember it that way for my own benefit. I genuinely remember Daphne and her friends insisting on going out dancing at a gay bar because they found it non-threatening and filled with fun music. Relationships are built on trust and I have no reason not to trust Daphne's word on that one.

We arrived at the party zone with what seemed like the entire province with us. There were rows upon rows of people, all clamouring to get a spot that had a clear view of the temporary screens that had been erected.

"I don't think I've ever seen this many people in one place."

Daphne just laughed.

"What?"

"Last year. You saw this many people last year. In this very spot."

I had already forgotten the Winter Olympics. It had barely been a year since they had overtaken the city and they were already forgotten as old news. That's how it goes I guess. So much for marking names forever into history. When I can't even remember experiencing something as grand as the Olympics, perhaps my perception and retention of the human experience is lacking.

Daphne would never say that, but I could tell it from her eyes that she thought it sometimes. The way that I could apparently miss the most obvious things drove her crazy. It wasn't that I was absent minded or lacked attention, it was just that the things that my mind chose to capture didn't always correspond with what she considered important. I suppose that is one place where we will forever be forced to disagree. I like to think that my mind has maintained its ability to recall significant events. It just seems that what was significant to me at different times may have been different than what other people, especially Daphne, expected.

"Oh yeah."

Daphne just laughed again.

"How many people do you think this is? One million? Two million?"

"You're helpless. There isn't anywhere near one million people here. It's closer to one hundred thousand."

"I am helpless, aren't I?"

I looked at her with my playful eyes and she smiled back with a flirtatious grin. The kind of cutting grin that was both affectionate and mischievous.

"Yeah, you are."

The game itself was torture. I had already seen three games where the Canucks had lost embarrassingly to the Bruins. The fourth really was the nail in the coffin. How could such a perfect season come to a close? How did the best team in the league let the title slip away? How could they let it happen that way? I was never fully able to comprehend what happened. It was a tragedy.

The real tragedy followed. Or maybe it started near the end. It is all a blur in hindsight, but I remember the sound of broken glass and the smell of smoke. The crackle of glass piercing my ears and the sooty aroma of anger and frustration wafting across my nose. It turned the party zone into ground zero. The shift happened immediately. The looters and hooligans appeared out of nowhere, seemingly taking the place of the very people that I had just spent the last few hours partying with. Instead of high-fives, I was worried about punches. What had they done with my friends? I'll never know that answer.

Daphne clung to me, as if I were some great protector and not the worthless slab of meat that my life up until that point had defined me as. It was a welcome embrace, a momentary shift in my existential role. I stopped being just another boyfriend and I had to become a bodyguard. She was the most important thing to me and my life and it didn't take an epiphany for me to realise that. I had to do everything in my power to ensure her safety.

The crowds started pushing and punches were being thrown. My mind was reeling. I didn't know what to think. Why are you doing this to yourself, Vancouver? Why? I heard the sound of a gunshot. Did that happen or did I imagine it? It must have happened, or something like that. Something that was so sudden and frightening that it might as well have been a gunshot. Fire was ablaze all around us. The flames crackling, burning up the remnants of our home. Daphne was beginning to shed tears. They were small, but I could tell that the city she had spent her entire life loving had finally broken her heart. Where was that civic pride for the world's most liveable city?

Smack. We were lying on the ground. I don't know who or what had collided with us, but Daphne and I lay on the asphalt with chaos surrounding us. I remember hearing the sound of people running in all directions and boots marching. Did I imagine that too?

I looked into Daphne's eyes and saw that she was genuinely scared for her life. With nothing else at my disposal, I chose then and there to pour all my love into her. I pushed her hair out of her face and planted my lips on hers. She was trembling, but receptive to my touch. I held her in my arms like the world was ending. It seemed like it was. It seemed as if everything about our hometown had betrayed us and was willing to drag us down into the same inferno that had taken to the streets.

"I love you."

"I love you, too."

48

I want that image to be burned into my mind forever. If there was ever a crystallised moment to keep, I want it to be that one. I want it to be two lovers, lying on the street in an embrace while hell opens up around them. That should be the defining moment of what all humanity is – a persistent refusal to give up on love.

How could the world end if there were once lovers like us?

July 1, 1999

I ran after Collette as if my legs depended on it. I was surprised with how fast she was. She didn't look it. She was a thin girl, with barely a hint of flesh on her boney frame. I didn't mind how petite she was. She still managed to gather up enough fat to form two tiny pert breasts that she let me touch. Most of the time it was over the fabric of her shirt, but on two different (special) occasions, she let my hands slide underneath and she'd undo her bra and I could feel her warm summer skin reach its peak at her nipples.

We didn't date for long. I don't recall how long it was in sum, perhaps three months. That sounds about right for a fourteen year old version of myself. It sounded right for a twenty year old version of me, too. But Collette wasn't around anymore when I was twenty. She had long moved on.

Collette had gone to university and met the love of her life. I think his name was Jared or Jarrod or Jarren. He was a tall fellow, if I remember correctly. Perhaps it was because Collette was so short that I thought of her Jared or Jarrod or Jarren as tall. In any case, Collette met him almost immediately upon arriving at UBC and I think they may have even been engaged by the time I was twenty (she would have been twenty-one). We eventually lost touch, Collette and I, and I never did find out whether she and Jared or Jarrod or Jarren had kids, but I like to think that they did.

Flying back in time, before her husband that I can't recall his name, back to our mid-teen years, Collette and I had a brief and delightful time together. It may have only been that one summer, but it was an amazing one. We would run after each other in playful glee. You might have even called it a frolic. I think it must have been the last real summer I ever had. I think it was that summer. Maybe it was the year after. It's hard to recall now, but I always liked looking back at my time with Collette and thinking that it was the zenith of my youth. Or perhaps it was my youth's nadir. When I was fourteen I didn't know what either of those words meant. I'm not entirely convinced that I know now.

50

We would run after each other, making a battlefield out of the park just to the east of White Rock beach. I think it was called Semiahmoo Park. It was just past the municipal boundaries, but I wasn't entirely sure whether it was part of Surrey or if it was native land. Nobody called it Semiahmoo Park, if that was its proper name. It was just the "Whale" Park, due to the underwhelming landmark of a children's slide shaped like an Orca that rested in the playground. It was this old ugly thing made of concrete with a tubular slide that started at the blow hole and exited at the mouth. I think it is long since gone. They may have removed it not too many years after that last summer. It was definitely gone before I graduated high school. Apparently the junkies liked to shoot up nearby and syringes had been found in the whale. Naturally, the best response to dealing with drug addiction was to destroy a children's playground.

Next to the park was a restaurant that changed names and owners and over the years became a go-to destination for more high-end diners, or at least that's the way I remember it. I believe Mom and Dad went there a few times with Mom's work. When I was fourteen, I think it was still a dump and attached to the restaurant, possibly around the back, was an arcade that I was forbidden from going to. I don't know what sort of dangers I was being protected from, but supposedly White Rock's seediest elements liked to frequent the arcade. These might have been the same junkies that used the whale slide as an injection site.

It wasn't that it really mattered, I guess, my not being allowed to go to an arcade. Mine was a generation that had been raised outside the arcade. We were children of the home console. I remember always having a Nintendo (the original one) in my home for as long as I was conscious. There were great Blades of Steel battles and World Cup 1990 victories. World Cup was fun because the playing surface could change (I believe it included ice, grass, sand, and a rocky terrain). Players could be knocked out of play with a hard kick of the ball (it turned into an unstoppable projectile), or if they tripped on an obstacle in the landscape (in that rocky terrain, for example).

None of those games compared to Wheel of Fortune, which Ashley and I spent half our childhood playing. I don't think I ever watched the television show, which was probably ultra-boring, but I knew almost every puzzle held in that 8-bit cartridge. It didn't mean that I never lost. It was challenging enough trying to buzz in correctly with those clunky controllers, or to slide the cursor over the correct letter. Ashley derived great pleasure in watching me fail to win my dream prize at the end. I remember that they let you choose before what you wanted to play for. Ashley would always choose something conventional like a sports car or a ski vacation. I chose the dining room suite.

Our generation moved on to other consoles and by the time I was fourteen I think I was firmly established as a PlayStation owner. I would play the updated versions of my old favourites, now NHL '98 and World Cup 1998 and laugh at the primitive nature of the NES.

My, how far we've come since.

I don't know why, but I never did find a suitable replacement for the Wheel of Fortune game. Maybe it was that a part of me was fine playing 1987's version forever. There was something kitsch and silly about the whole thing. It was analogous to almost everything I enjoyed in life. It took a bit of effort after a while. We'd have to blow on those cartridges just to get them to maybe work, and even then there was the possibility of the game crashing before I could take home a new executive kitchenette. Dad would bring out the air compressor and try to scare every last speck of dust out, but even that never seemed to fully work in the end.

Collette was a Nintendo64 owner when we dated and could (virtually) beat me single-handedly at any game in her collection. I wanted to blame it on some freak ability she had. Like she was some sort of mutant with the power to communicate with electronics. I wanted to blame it on the odd three-pronged shape of the 64 controller, which will go down in video game history as the least ergonomically designed controller ever. Who had three thumbs? I wanted to blame it on all the hours of extra practice she had as an owner. The truth was, I couldn't ever focus straight on the game when I was with Collette.

I just kept thinking about when the next opportunity would be for me to put my hands on her breasts. It was a simple dream of mine. I don't think it ever truly evolved past that point when I was fourteen. I guess, deep down, I had always just wanted to hold breasts in my hands. It might have been my calling on this planet. With Collette, I would hold out hope that whatever day it was would be a special occasion and she would let me slide underneath her shirt and I'd be able to feel the warmth again. I wanted to touch those mysterious ridges so badly I couldn't ever drive a MarioKart right.

At the Whale Park, Collette would jump on the merry-go-round and I would grab the bar and give us a spin. I'd lean over and press my foot into the red, dusty sand and get us started. I'd pump my leg as much as I could and then lift it up and let the force turn us around wildly. The trees would turn into blurs of evergreen. Collette would sit in the middle of the carousel and close her eyes. I could never close my eyes because I knew that if I did I would get sick. I would focus on nothing in particular and let all the blurred colours – the evergreen trees, the orange slides, the blue sky – twirl around until they slowed enough for me to recognise them again. I'd let the merry-go-round come to a stop at its own pace while my stomach readjusted to normal speed and force. We weren't astronauts, but the centrifugal force I felt made me feel that I was somewhat qualified to be shot up into the sky.

"Want to watch the fireworks?"
"Yeah."

Though it was a small town (or city, if one insists upon actual, legal titles), White Rock always managed to put together a magnificent fireworks display in those days. The beach was a perfect location to hold them because the town was built on a slope that faced in its direction. Nearly everyone would be able to see the fireworks from home. But home was the worst place to watch. To really experience the fireworks, and I mean to really experience them, meant lying down on the grass mere metres away from where the municipal workers lit them off.

The sound was deafening and the smell of gunpowder filled the nostrils for days.

It smelled of summer. It was as natural as the scent of salt water or fish and chips.

"Can you see any shooting stars?"
"No. But I'll let you know if I do."

The first stream of fireworks went off. Pop, pop, pop, went the display. They were green, blue and red and they exploded outwards in a standard circular motion.

"I think I saw one."

Collette gripped my hand. It was warm, but not clammy. Reassuring, but never clingy.

My favourite fireworks appeared halfway through the display. It must have been about 10:08pm – the show was always fifteen minutes long. They were the ones that shot out and disappeared into the sky after the sound. Just when you've almost lost hope in their existence, they reappear and spin around in a mesmerising counter-clockwise spiral fashion.

"I like those ones, Collette."
"Me too."

Long after the crowds had dispersed, Collette and I were curled up on the grass. She wore my kangaroo hoodie and looked adorable. My arms wrapped around her and slid underneath the sweatshirt and rested on her stomach. I could feel her pierced navel, the metal stud cold against my fingertips, providing a stark contrast to the heat her body was producing.

"Did you want to?"

A firework shot out, disappearing into the sky.

"Want to what?"
"Nevermind."

I let the moment pass without pressing to feel more of her. I don't remember who broke up with whom, but by September we would no longer be together and my hands would ache for another opportunity to rest up against a navel piercing, let alone a firm nipple.

July 4, 2003

"You are awful!"

Martin had made a rude comment at Jade and she had reacted as any reasonable person ought to. I said nothing as I hadn't actually seen much at fault at what Martin had said. I don't know if that made me unreasonable or if it just meant that years of being friends with Martin had desensitised me to his type of humour. I didn't think that he was actually a mean person at his core. He just had a bit of a bite. He was the kind of person that if you knew him you'd love him, but if you didn't know him you'd think that he was a jerk, which again, I don't think he actually was.

"Can you believe him?"

Jade had dragged me away from the group because she wanted to get a bit of fresh air. It seemed that whatever space Martin was occupying was sucking up all the oxygen. I didn't feel that way, but I had no problem being someone that my friends could vent to. We walked along the sand, letting the soggy twigs crackle beneath our feet under the moonlight.

"Yeah, I know."

I didn't know. I hadn't noticed what was so bad about Martin or his comment. I barely noticed those sort of things. I guess that was a fault that I needed to work on. In the meantime I would just nod in agreement with my friends. I would act concerned. I would show that I knew what was going on. I just wanted to pretend like I did. In the end, I had no idea what to say.

I wasn't sure why I was struggling for words, but maybe it was that time in our lives. There were certain moments that everything hinged on. This was the last summer of our youth. For real, that is. While most of us had long had to give into working our summers away, this was the last one before we were expected to contribute something to society. I guess I expected that to be the point when everything would make sense. I thought perhaps when you reach adulthood there was no need for a guidebook, it just came naturally.

We had all graduated from high school just a few weeks previous and it was only starting to sink in that it was real as the summer came quickly and reminded us how short it usually stuck around. We had gone to English Bay for Canada Day and managed to lose one of our friends in the crowds and confusion. Martin had found it hilarious, and I did too. Rodney, the friend that we lost didn't find it as amusing, though he was generally a good sport.

We had all taken the SkyTrain from Scott Road in North Delta to downtown and decided to walk down Denman street. In the madness, we were broken into a couple of smaller groups. Somewhere in all of that, Rodney was lost. Of everyone in the group as a whole, he was the only one who still didn't have a cell phone. Even if we had wanted to get a hold of him, we wouldn't have had a chance.

Was it Jade that had the bright idea of calling Rodney's parents to see if he had checked in?

It wasn't such a bright idea. It made them worry about the ability of their eighteen year old son to not disappear. If parents were already hesitant about the readiness of their children to enter the world upon high school graduation, getting lost from your friends the one time you head downtown doesn't help. They didn't freak out, but I could tell that they were certainly concerned. We promised to have him call home, if, when we got a hold of Rodney.

We all felt terrible. We walked up and down the beach, looking for him. Where had he gone? How could we really lose someone when there was a group of us? Didn't someone see him pop off? You would have thought someone would have noticed him missing sooner. I would have noticed if Martin wasn't beside me. What did that say about how much I cared about Rodney? After covering every stretch of real estate we could conceive of, we boarded the SkyTrain dejected.

Rodney's stupid grin greeted us at Scott Road station.

"There you are!"

"Yeah."

"We thought we had lost you."

"You did."

"What are you doing here?"

"It made sense that you'd all have to return to your cars."

"When did you come back here?"

"Almost right away."

"Did you see the fireworks?"

He hadn't. Just a few days later we were down at White Rock Beach watching the Independence Day fireworks from Blaine. Even though Blaine was a tiny town, its fireworks put the Canada Day celebrations in Vancouver to shame, to say nothing of what little old White Rock pulled off each year.

Off on our little walk, Jade took my hand and looked into my eyes.

"You know that I like you, right?"

I was shocked. I had no idea that Jade had liked me at all. I had thought all the time she spent bickering with Martin was a form of flirtation. I had felt there was some sort of primal connection between them that maybe they didn't even realise. I thought that eventually they would succumb to that desire and couple off.

"Um, no. I didn't know that."

"I just wanted to let you know that."

"Okay."

Jade let my hand go and turned to face the water. The tide was in. The moon's reflection was lighting up the waves. I could see piles of kelp floating in front of us.

"Do you want to go for a swim?"

Before I could respond, Jade started walking forward into the cold, salty Pacific. My eyes watched in disbelief. Before I knew what had come over me, my knees were wet. Then my waist. Then my shoulders. It didn't take much for the water to drop off and for my entire body to be submerged. There was something peaceful about the consistency of the tides and knowing that they would be with us now, go away for a while, and come back again, like clockwork. I let my head dunk below a cresting wave and popped back up for air.

"It's nice, isn't it?"

"Yeah, it's not so bad."

"I'm sorry for making you uncomfortable just then."

"You didn't make me uncomfortable."

"I did. I just wanted to say sorry."

I let the moment pass as it was. She hadn't made me uncomfortable at all. I don't think that would have been possible for her. In another time and place, Jade and I could have been something. We might have even been something special. She was fun and quirky and our personalities meshed well. I don't know why I had never noticed her much before. Nothing ever came of us. We just bobbed up and down, using our arms and legs keep us afloat. The moon kept watch over its tides.

Jade didn't need to explain herself any further and she didn't. She was leaving for university in Ontario at the end of the summer and I guess I could tell that she was content with never finding out what would come between us. She just needed to let me know. It was strange thinking that. It was strange, but comforting. That there would always be that bond. I guess maybe that was what she had intended. To create a bond that we would always have. Maybe not, I don't know. It's dangerous business supposing what other people mean. I don't try to do it often. I just thought there might have been something in what Jade had felt the need to share. She had kept it to herself for years and from what I could tell, she had kept it from the rest of the group as well.

Martin and I had always suspected that Jade had spent her time pining over him. We would hang out a lot, just the two of us, and play video games and chat about stuff. One of our topics of discussion was the degree to which Jade liked him. I don't know why I never asked him why he hadn't made a move. I think he was just hoping that one day she would come to him and ask him out. Out in the water, I couldn't help but think of Martin. It was a small victory that I would never be able to hold over him. Not openly, anyways.

As she treaded water in front of me, I think I saw the starlight in Jade's eyes and wanted her to place her lips on mine then and there. If nothing more should ever come between us, we might always have that one kiss. It never came.

Rodney was being teased mercilessly by Martin when we returned to the group to the point that a song was being written about Rodney getting lost in Vancouver. Martin strummed a basic progression on his guitar, belting out the words. Erik and Louise were laughing. Rodney just watched on in a neutral expression. I couldn't tell whether he was the brunt of our jokes or we were actually the brunt of his. Had he been playing games with us forever? There was always that uneasiness that perhaps, despite what we had seen and heard, Rodney might have been the smartest one of us all.

"Rodney got lost, la la la."

The chorus repeated like that, over and over. I can't remember all the words. Erik provided backup to Martin's lead vocals.

The bonfire burned in front of us and we revelled in its illegal existence. The crackling of wet driftwood. The thick smoke it exhaled. As far as most of us had experienced throughout our teenage years, if you tucked yourself far enough down the beach, so that you were most probably on native land, it usually wouldn't have been an issue. The further away from

59

the restaurants and bars, the better. We rarely brought alcohol with us, so the appearance of a ranger would have been a mild concern.

The worst I had experienced had been with a different group of friends and glass bottles had been brought with us. We weren't being rowdy, but we did laugh and imbibe. We let ourselves enjoy the fullness of our youth. As we sighted the flashlight making its rounds down the beach, moving towards us, we quietly found a nearby log to stuff our beers behind and returned to our fire. I guess we thought we were fine, but Derek had forgotten to get rid of one of his empties. He tossed the bottle away into the bushes and the sound of broken glass hastened our visit from the patrolling officer.

He never did see any beer around us, but he did instruct us to put out our campfire which effectively ended our night.

On this particular night, it was quiet. Jade wrapped herself in a towel and let the heat of the fire dry her off from her swim. I tried to do the same, but due to the wind, I kept getting smoke in my eyes and it was becoming too uncomfortable to dry off. I stood up to get out of the way of the breeze. It was quite cold to my skin, as the salty beads dripped down my legs.

Living the closest to the beach, and having my car parked not too far away, I said I was just going to pop home and grab a change of clothes.

"No, you don't have to go, do you?"

"I don't, no. I just want to get warm."

"If you go, you know that we're all going to go and then the night is over."

"I guess so."

Jade looked at me with those starlit eyes and scooted slightly to the side and made a glance that I was to platonically warm up next to her. I plopped myself down and let the warmth of the (smokeless) fire dry me off.

December 31, 2006

I stood bored on the side of the room. I never really liked Carrie's friends. They all seemed to wear a smug sense of urban superiority to those of us from the 'burbs. I don't know if they even knew that they had it. Carrie couldn't tell it was that way. Of course, Carrie was infected with it, too. I did my best not to let it bother me, but for all my luck, it wasn't going to disappear as long as I lived at Mom and Dad's house in White Rock and it wasn't as if that moving downtown would forever rid me of the naïveté of White Rock.

"Where did you go to high school?"

It was a stupid question that people in their twenties should stop asking of each other, as if the place you spent your formative teenage years actually mattered. They would never recognise the name of my school, anyways. It was nowhere to them. I was from nowhere. Even if the school I came from was more than adequate. In fact, it was much better than that. It was an exceptional school. However, it was as if anything that made it special or gave it a claim to fame escaped the attention of the Point Grey bubble. Maybe it did. Maybe there really was something special about the West End.

"No, I don't think I've heard of that one."

An expression of boredom crosses their face at the mere mention of an unknown entity, which I've now confirmed myself as being. I was an unknown entity from nowhere. Whatever was I doing at this party? Who could have brought such a nobody? Carrie had brought me, of course. But, I had no idea where my girlfriend was. Carrie was nowhere to be seen, as she had been swept away by her closest friends, probably to gossip in the upstairs bathroom, or sneak cigarettes on the driveway.

Carrie wasn't a smoker, as far as I knew. I just kept catching her smoking. It probably demanded an explanation, but that was never the nature of our relationship. She would determine the boundaries that were, and most importantly, were not up for discussion. I guess she had decided that her mysterious interest in tobacco was in the latter category. Based on the unspoken rules, I was to leave it at that, and so I did for the most part. I mean, I didn't say anything to Carrie, but I did let it eat away at me from the inside, almost like some sort of cancer. It wouldn't have bothered me so much if it wasn't for the fact that I detested smoking and smokers and would never date one in a million years. I guess that fact led me to believe, by extension (and disbelief) that Carrie wasn't a smoker.

There is little that a stranger can do at a party on their own. They can help themselves to the buffet and they can stand around and look awkward, two tasks that I was excelling in. I was pretty good at standing around and looking awkward on my own, for that I needed no practice, this was just display time. Buffets weren't really part of my normal routine, but I was discovering that I had a natural talent for them. Marius, the Slovak Boy Wonder (as I secretly called him) came to keep me company.

I called Marius the Slovak Boy Wonder in large part due to his being of Eastern European origin (he could have been Latvian for all I knew) and for possessing the remarkable ability to be both six feet seven inches tall and unable to grow any facial hair.

"Hi."

"Hey."

"Cool party, yeah?"

"Yeah, cool party."

"You come to these a lot?"

I couldn't tell whether Marius was hitting on me or actually just struggling to make conversation. Of course I didn't come to these a lot. It was a New Year's Eve party. My basic knowledge of them were that they happened once per year. It wasn't that I had a significant amount of experience that would eclipse anyone else's at the party. As far as I could tell, we had all experienced the passing of time at roughly the same pace.

"Um, no. I guess this is my first time here."

I decided to play it cool and assume that Marius was just curious about whether I had gone to any of the other parties the erstwhile hosts had put on. Being a student house and not someone's parents' home, I suspected that keggers and Jello shot parties were regular occurrences, along with strippers and cocaine and everything else that rich university students got up to.

"It's a nice place, no?"

"Yeah, it is."

The student housing was nicer than the home I grew up in. That was a depressing thought to have. I don't think that affluence is all that important. There is probably a certain level of it that once you pass it the rest is all bonus and you barely notice anymore. Maybe not. It was a poor theory I had based on absolutely no actual knowledge. I didn't come from an affluent family, though we weren't poor either. We were just middle class. Maybe not just middle class, but a certain kind of middle class. We were the aspirational type that looked forward to moving up the socioeconomic ladder with time, but still being firmly routed in a working-class background. If my family was going to climb the ladder, chances are we were going to have to do a bit of manual labour along the way.

I thought of the tiled mirrored wall my parents tore down on the day they were able to buy the home they had rented for years. It had been a hideous "feature wall", but it had provided hours of amusement, in that I couldn't help but admire myself. I wasn't vain, I didn't think, I just knew that I was a really good looking boy and any girl would be lucky to spend her life with me.

Where was Carrie? Where was the love of my life? Where, oh where, had my girlfriend gone. It was New Year's Eve and I thought it most appropriate that she be by my side. I was getting sick of Marius. I was sick of his smooth skin the moment he came galloping over to my side. I hated his suspenders. I hated that he was wearing a slim fit suit that would never suit my frame. I hated that he was hovering above me with his great Giraffe-like height. I wanted to grab a step ladder so he'd stop leaning in to talk to me. Give me some space, Marius!

"Have you seen Carrie?"

"Carrie? Carrie?"

His dumb face thought long and hard about the question I had asked. I wasn't sure if he was struggling to decide whether he knew where Carrie was or if he actually didn't know who Carrie was. I knew that he knew Carrie. That was how I knew Marius, through Carrie.

We had gone for dinner, a group of us, I think it was sushi, possibly Korean barbeque, and Marius was introduced to me for the first time. I had met most of Carrie's high school friends before, but Marius was more like a caricature that I had only heard of in amusing anecdotes. Someone that I didn't believe to be real until I met him for that first time and was shocked to see that he existed.

He ordered sushi the way that you would have imagined a sumo wrestler ordering sushi. By the time he was finished ordering, I was so confused about what I wanted that I made the awful mistake of just saying to the waiter that I would have the same. Ninety dollars later and possibly five pounds heavier, I left the restaurant.

"No, I don't know."

Even his answer didn't clear up what I thought he might have been battling internally. I excused myself and went into the kitchen to grab some pop from the fridge. I had decided to stay sober so I could borrow my Dad's car. I figured public transit from Vancouver to White Rock was a nightmare at the best of times, it would be far worse on New Year's.

Sober on New Year's. That was the true nightmare. Being forced to listen to awful stories by uninteresting drunk people I didn't know. It only got worse when they reverted to telling inside jokes and laughing hysterically, even though the "joke" part of the inside joke had long disappeared from the retelling. Nobody understands you! Wait, no, everyone understands you! I don't! It's not fair!

They laughed like hyenas. I stood dumbfounded that anyone could consider these people worthy of friendship. I thought of my friends from high school and missed them. We hadn't really been gathered in a group for years. It was a shame that I felt inside, that I had let a group of amazing individuals slip away so that I could chase imaginary girls who left me with their unbearable friends.

Carrie wasn't imaginary. I just had no confirmation that she existed based on the majority of the evening. I looked at my watch to see how much more of this I would be forced to endure. I hated New Year's because it has a built-in deadline that everyone must at least stick around for. You can't excuse yourself at ten-thirty to head home. You must cheer in the New Year. You must. We mustn't forget to cheer in the New Year. You can't miss that. It's not like it will be there for much longer. I could care less about 2007. I would have 365 days to get used to it being there, and countless more to recall it until the ends of time.

I wanted to stand with Carrie by my side, triumphantly. I wanted these jerks to see that none of them won. I won. All of them had gone to high school with her, but in her adult wisdom had found someone from outside Point Grey. She had found a guy from the suburbs they so detested. I wasn't sure if they detested the suburbs, I just was more certain that they had never been. I wasn't even sure that they had a firm grasp on where geographically White Rock was in comparison to their home. White Rock was just a name on exit signs on Highway 99. They probably barely noticed when they were passing by on their way to Seattle.

Ours was just an imaginary place without any consequence to them. I wish that wasn't true, but how could I really believe that if even I would eventually leave. We all did. The reasons to stay became fewer and fewer, and those that stayed had to contend with the challenges of exponentially rising housing costs and long commutes into the city, where they, like the rest of us, had been drawn for work.

If society had fled to the suburbs in the 1950s, it was ready to reverse course in the early 2000s.

I hadn't yet moved to the city by then. I was still one of the many moochers who escaped the awful cost of living by having to bear the non-financial burden of family. It was a tiring arrangement as I tried to assert myself as an independent adult, but no matter how you cut it, I wasn't really all that independent. Mom and Dad still paid for my food and accommodations, most of my transportation, and rather indicatively, my tuition – the very ticket that most of us used as an excuse to flee home.

That night, as I stood in the kitchen, drinking a flat soda, hamstrung by the responsibility of automobile driving, I drew the conclusion that I needed to leave home. I would leave White Rock. I would flee to the city to be with the youth. I would become part of what was happening and leave behind everything that had happened. Cities were for the living. Suburbs were for the dead.

I swear it wasn't that I had just gotten sick of trying to explain to people exactly where I lived, even if it was only half an hour away. There was far more to it than that. I think petty annoyance is hardly a reason to pick up stakes and move. I think you need something a bit more than that. In any case, it wasn't like moving to the city would create some new roots for me that would be accepted by the landed gentry of Point Grey. I would always have the mark of someone who was born and raised in the suburbs. It just became clear that it was time to go.

"Hey hon."

Carrie found me in the kitchen and wrapped her arms around my waist, her broad face smiling back at me. It was such a welcome embrace. If ever there was a need for someone to reassure me that I wasn't a nobody from nowhere, it was at that moment, just before the clocks and calendars would reach their peak and then reset again to zero.

"How's it going?"

"Not bad. You?"

"I think I'm a little bit tipsy."

"Oh."

"You aren't mad, are you?"

I was.

"No. It's fine."

"Are you sure? I know you said that you weren't drinking because you had to drive, but I didn't think that it necessarily meant that I had to not drink too, right? Cuz I think that isn't necessary, right? I hope you aren't mad."

She rambled as I held her closer to my chest, hoping that sweet, guileless affection would eventually shut her up. Of course I didn't like being sober. But I was. I didn't like being the only person not from Point Grey at the party. But I was. They were unchanging situations that my intoxicated girlfriend wasn't going to be able to solve.

At the strike of midnight, I think we were all gathered outside on the back porch, where it was surprisingly mild, maybe ten or fifteen degrees. Pots and pans were being banged with wooden spoons. Carrie planted her fulsome lips on me and I could taste the gin she had been imbibing.

"Happy New Year."

"Happy New Year."

I wanted to imagine growing old with Carrie in some large Kerrisdale house. We could have had a big mangy mutt that our kids would love. But as I wrapped my arms around her and closed my eyes for the briefest of seconds, I could see that it was a fleeting fantasy. This was never going to be forever. I think I knew that then. I just didn't know how many grains of sand were in the hourglass.

Before I drove back to the suburbs, I took Carrie in my car and found a parking lot by Spanish Bank.

December 31, 2005

Drinks were being offered all around. I declined as I had decided to borrow my Dad's car for the evening. It didn't bother me all that much, New Year's Eve was fairly overrated anyways. How many times are we going to celebrate this? What was important was surrounding oneself with friends. It had been a long time, but I was thrilled when Martin invited me to his apartment for the little gathering he was hosting.

It wasn't much, a few snacks and some pop and beer in the fridge, but it was welcoming and I had so much I needed to catch up with from almost everyone at the party. I had really wanted to catch up with Rodney, especially. I don't know why that was. It might have been because I was curious to see what an adult version of him actually looked and functioned as. It was disappointing to discover that he wasn't at Martin's party that night. I don't know why he wasn't there. Maybe he had other plans. Maybe he didn't really like Martin. Maybe he got lost. Aside from Rodney, the rest of the gang was there.

Erik was someone that I hadn't seen in probably two, maybe two and a half years. He looked terrific, he really did. I think he must have lost about twenty pounds. He was always the guy who was carrying a bit of baby weight, all through high school and then came into his own as an adult. I asked him about what he was up to and he explained to me about his apprenticeship. It was something to do with electricity, but he insisted that he wasn't becoming an electrician. I forget the exact details of what it was he did, but I do remember how firm he was that it wasn't the same as being an electrician.

In any case, it was nice to see him. We had never been close, but we had always been friendly. I don't know if everyone saw me that way, but that's how I'd like to think that they did. I would love to have been remembered that way, if people remember me at all.

Whatever became of them all?

Erik and Louise had apparently broken up just after high school, but they were still on good terms, I guess, as Louise had brought her new (current?) boyfriend to Martin's party. He was a really nice guy, more than a little bit older, someone that she had met at the university. Was he a graduate student? He might have even been a junior professor, come to think of it. He looked like a man who had lived at least a decade more than us. It didn't really bother me. He made Louise happy, I could tell that. I noticed that he and Erik seemed to chat quite casually about hockey, so it wasn't like there was any burning tension in the room, but it's not like I would have noticed that anyways. I was terrible at keeping track of those sort of things.

Like Martin and Jade.

I hadn't known that they had even begun dating. That was news to me when I arrived at that New Year's Eve party. It was an utter shock when they used the occasion to announce their engagement.

"Congratulations!"

I looked at Jade and saw that she was genuinely happy. There was something authentic about the way that her smile effortlessly appeared. Martin beamed as he held his champagne flute high.

"I'm just so proud to say that Jade wants to spend the rest of her life with me."

Jade had gone to Waterloo for two school years and returned for the final two by transferring to Simon Fraser. I later learned that she and Martin had begun dating the summer between her first and second year university when they both worked at a summer camp. By the time they finally got married, Jade would put her Master's degree aside and devote her life to raising two beautiful boys, while Martin struggled to keep his dream of being a music producer afloat.

I didn't see them much after that New Year's party. I went to the wedding. It was a pleasant enough event, though I remember the reception hall being far too warm for my liking. I may have had far too much to drink and danced like a fool, but that is what weddings are about, you know, aside from the nuptials. I think I ran into Martin once afterwards in a grocery store. It was more than a few years later. He was balding, had let his body go quite a bit, and I noticed a coffee stain on the pocket of his shirt.

"It's a challenge, but it's a wonderful one."

I don't remember if he was talking about his career, his wife, or his kids, but I remember being envious of him. It sounded like his life was tiring and the effects could be read by looking at him. His life was full, though. It was a complete life, the kind that real men were meant to live. Martin was living the dream.

I stood on Martin's balcony and surveyed the view.

"It's nice, isn't it?"

Jade stood at the door, holding two champagne flutes.

"It is. It is really nice out."

I smiled at her warmly and accepted the glass, though I only really sipped from it once or twice. I was still concerned about remaining sober for the drive home. I was young and stupid, but I wasn't reckless.

"You looked shocked in there."
"I guess I was."

Jade grinned.

"Life is funny, isn't it?"
"Hilarious."

"Do you know how Martin asked me out?"

"No."

"I was life guarding at the camp and he came down to the dock with his cabin of boys. I overheard one of them dare him to ask me out."

"Really?"

She laughed, closing her eyes and shaking her head. It just wobbled back and forth in a real casual manner, as if she had done that motion a million times before. When she finished, the moonlight bounced off her eyes, reminding me of the time we swam together. It was as if Jade would always be connected to the night for me. I don't really remember any conversations we had during daytime. I know they happened. We had been friends for years. I certainly recall hanging out with her during the day, at least abstractly. I just couldn't remember any particular time when we had a meaningful conversation with the sun still up. It was actually as if the moon controlled the severity of Jade's conversations, like emotional tidal patterns.

"I said no to him. He was shocked. All that time he had thought that I had loved him, or something."

I tried to force a smile to my face. I thought immediately of all the times that Martin and I had sat around and talked about Jade. I wondered if he had shared that fact with her. Couples share pretty much everything. Was I now the one on the outside looking in? I had always thought that Martin and I were the ones with the secrets together. How did he manage to hide the fact that he and Jade had been dating for almost two years from me? Had I been that blind? No, I hadn't been blind, I just hadn't been around. Drifting, drifting, I was always drifting.

"It burned him up inside, I guess. He kept coming up to me, this time without any kids around, and asking again. I think he could best be described as begging for me to go out with him. Finally, I said yes. On our day off, we took a canoe over to the town and grabbed some gelato."

"When did you know?"

"I knew, for sure, the third time he asked me."

"That's quite persistent."

"I just wanted to know he was serious."

Jade took a sip of her champagne. She looked out over the skyline and smiled. I didn't understand why she smiled so often. Perhaps she really was happy. That was hard to comprehend. In my experience, at least, happiness has been a series of fleeting moments. Why did they not flee from Jade? What was her secret that allowed her to hoard happiness? Maybe she didn't hoard happiness, that sounds mean. She had decided to share some of it with Martin.

"How about you? Any ladies out there?"

"No, nothing right now."

She nodded, gave a quick wink and headed back inside to join her fiancé. That was the end of our last moonlit conversation ever. We would never really have another time when we could chat at night. Life moved on. Jade got married. I kept drifting. At the door, Jade turned to me and spoke the most haunting words I had ever heard.

"Yours will come along. I believe that. You just have to be persistent."

September 3, 1996

Mrs. Chow read off the attendance list with great interest. I hated the first day of school. It was the end of the summer. I had just spent the past three months reading Austen and Dickens, what could they force me to learn this year that would be more worthwhile?

"Sergey Golding?"

"Here."

Everyone turned their heads to look at the strange boy who had arrived from out of nowhere. He was peculiar looking and seemed to have a funny accent.

"Are you new, Sergey?"

"Yes, ma'am."

"Where do you come from?"

"Um, well, originally from Russia, but more recently from Australia."

"Oooh, Australia, that is so interesting! Isn't it class? We have a real Aussie in our class!"

I could tell that it was going to be a very long year if Mrs. Chow was going to be our teacher. I could also tell that rather than correct her, Sergey had adopted the strategy of just going with whatever flow Mrs. Chow created. Even if it was patently stupid.

"Did you have a pet kangaroo?"

Malcolm, possibly the stupidest kid in the class, but notably the most physically mature, was the interrogator. He had taken over from where Mrs. Chow had left off. Apparently, this class was turning into a question and answer forum and we hadn't even got through the attendance list.

"Uh, no. We lived in the suburbs."

Mrs. Chow's eyes lit up.

"Oh, I didn't know they had suburbs in Australia!"

Sergey let his face show disappointment.

"Australia is pretty much exactly like Canada, except they have different accents and their video games don't work here."

Mrs. Chow let her face show disappointment.

"Oh, well. I had always wanted to go. I guess I need not bother, now."
"Francis Harriman?"
"Present."
"Are you new, Francis?"
"Yes, Mrs. Chow. I moved here from Mississauga, Ontario. Would you like to hear all about it?"
"No, maybe some other time, Francis, I need to get through the rest of this list."

Francis let his face show disappointment. I could tell that he was really excited to tell us all about the wonders of suburban Toronto.

At recess I decided to take the opportunity to chat with Sergey and Francis, as most of the other kids were catching up with their friends from last year.

"So, you're Russian, right?"
"Yeah."
"Does that mean that we hate you?"

Francis was demonstrating that the Ontario education system was not, in fact, that much better than what British Columbia had been producing. I only had a small sample to go on, but I wasn't impressed.

"No, not any more. We're all friends now."

"Oh."

"Why did we hate you before?"

"Because the Soviet Union was communist."

Francis looked really confused.

"Where is the Soviet Union?"

"It doesn't exist anymore."

I tried to be as helpful as I could, but I realised as soon as the words left my mouth that the abstract idea of a country not existing any more might have been difficult for a slow learner to comprehend. It was more than apparent that Francis Harriman, formerly of Mississauga, Ontario, was a slow learner.

"Wait, where did it go?"

"It, well, it collapsed."

I remembered the encyclopedias and atlases that Mom and Dad had around the house that were outdated. I remember Dad pointing out countries that didn't exist anymore and laughing. There was no more Rhodesia or Siam, he would inform me.

"Like, all the buildings fell down and stuff?"

"No, not really. Basically, the type of government they had fell apart and they started from scratch again."

"So it still exists?"

"No. It's now called Russia."

I looked at Sergey to see if he agreed with my description.

"Yeah, pretty much. There are also a bunch of new countries, too. But the big one is still Russia. That is the part that I am from."

"I thought you were from Australia."

"I am, sort of. We lived in Australia for a while. Then we came here."

"Why?"

"Um, well, I don't know why. My parents told me they wanted to come to Canada because it would be better for their jobs and that maybe my grandparents can come live with us. I'd like that. It's been a long time since I've seen them."

"Why can't you visit them?"

"Well, at first we couldn't. We weren't allowed back into the Soviet Union and then when we were able to visit, it only happened not that often. It is really expensive to go to Russia to visit."

"Are you poor?"

"No."

"Why can't you visit your grandparents, then? I see mine all the time."

Francis was beginning to annoy both Sergey and I. I made eye contact with Sergey and just nodded in knowing agreement. Francis was hopeless, but ultimately harmless. We thought that we could humour him throughout recess and then probably ditch him with some other crowd of people. Amazingly enough, we did exactly that.

More amazing, I suppose, in the grand scheme of things, is that Francis turned out to be a much brighter kid than we suspected and hung out with us all the way through the end of elementary and even through high school. He eventually moved to New Zealand, I believe, and never came back. I don't know if he was able to afford to visit his grandparents from Wellington.

At lunch we sat by the playground and ate our sandwiches. Sergey had bologna. I had peanut butter and banana.

"Is everyone here stupid?"

I laughed. I had never really given it much thought before.

"Yeah. Pretty much."

Sergey smiled. I think he could tell that I was alright and that he wouldn't have to dumb down everything he said to speak to me. It wasn't like I was Mrs. Chow, sixth grade teacher.

"Good to know."

"So, what do you do for fun, seriously in Australia, if none of you have pet kangaroos?"

I smiled as I said it. I had learned that using sarcasm was a good way to express myself with the right audience.

"I really like playing video games. I read a bit, too. I like sci-fi. Do you like sci-fi?"

"A little, I guess. I don't really know a lot of it. I've read Lord of the Rings."

"That's fantasy, not sci-fi."

"Oh."

Sergey laughed.

"It's okay, not many people know the difference. I don't think you are dumb like the others."

I laughed a reassured laugh.

"That's good."

"How about you?"

"No, I don't think you are dumb, Sergey. Not at all."

He laughed and bit into his bologna sandwich.

"Is there anything worthwhile to do in this town?"
"No."

He just smiled and shook his head.

April 19, 2013

Eventually we all grow weary of home. Maybe it is something hard-wired in our genes, going back to the beginning of time, before we developed the ability of speech. Before we could be nagged to go. We would just know that it is time. That would be the sort of survival skill that Darwin would have found useful. I presume, of course, that Darwin was nagged by his mother. I don't know it to be true, but I wouldn't bet against it. A lot of great overachievers in history might have had that initial drive to succeed instilled in them from a young age.

As we get older, it becomes natural to move on. To find ourselves and establish a new life outside of the maternal nest. We meet other people who are also venturing out into the world alone and we pair off to settle down. Daphne and I had that for a while. Well, we had some approximation of that. It was just never complete, I guess, which is what caused her to leave. She wanted to settle down forever and I wasn't there yet. I didn't mind having our own apartments, even if we spent all our nights together. There was just something structurally reassuring about possessing an apartment lease taken out solely in your own name. I could always claim that it was my apartment. That was clear enough.

She left me to fend for myself. I was left with my apartment. There was something really depressing about knowing that after someone you had practically been living with for three years leaves no paper work required changing or updating. Did that make us any less real? I thought of people who had been in similar long term relationships and realised that I couldn't think of any that had dated for three years without eventually consolidating into a single shared apartment. I hadn't even thought of that as being an option for Daphne and I. Had I thought that we would go on forever in our current arrangement? I might have been happy that way. It seems kind of ridiculous to imagine a seventy year old man taking the Canada Line to spend the night at his seventy year old girlfriend's apartment. It would always be too soon, I guess. I don't know if Daphne thought that breaking up with me might be enough to cause me to change my ways. Maybe she thought a shock to my system would prepare me for that stage in life that we both ought to be.

Instead, I got a wild case of wanderlust after Daphne left me. There was nothing I wanted more than to fly far away from home. So the nest has been destroyed? Good. Let me fly. Let me go and see everything that the world has to offer. I am too young to settle down. Maybe later. Maybe when I am seventy we can talk about consolidation. I thought those things.

To be completely honest, I suffered from the exact opposite of that for a few weeks first. I had no desire to go anywhere but into the blackness. I wished there was a dark void then that I could disappear into for the rest of eternity. Pain ought to be erased or forgotten. I shouldn't have had to live through that.

I would lie in bed for days on end. All the accumulated sick days I had tallied began to disappear quickly. My boss said he'd have to fire me if I wasn't really sick. I thought that rather unfair. What could be more sick than losing one's life? Maybe not physically, but in every other aspect it was gone: emotionally, spiritually, sexually. I would even go so far as to say that it was gone physically, too. I missed her embrace. I missed her crocodile mug.

Rather than risk losing my employment, I returned to work. I showed up one day and pretended to be back to normal. I tried to go through the motions, to at least occupy my mind, if not please my employer. It became its own sort of nightmare. I was a zombie, living in a world that had no need for my dead body.

It was short-lived. I put in my two weeks' notice and moved back to Mom and Dad's home. I didn't even have that apartment in my name anymore. At least I didn't have to listen to my parents' annoying voicemail messages anymore. I got the live versions.

"How you feeling today?"

"Are you doing alright?"

"Did you want me to open these blinds a bit?"

"We were just going to have supper now, feel free to join us if you'd like."

I spent my twenty-eighth birthday alone, in bed. The next day I found an ice cream cake in the freezer with a note from Mom, just wanting me to know to "help myself." Real lovely, Mom. I didn't know if she meant for that note to have as many psychological layers as the cake. In reality, she probably meant well, and her choice of words was unfortunate.

On the top of the cake was a design in icing, the kind that parents usually get their (much) younger children. It was a dinosaur playing football. I guess Mom had asked if they had any with rugby on it. I guess the football was close enough, in terms of drawings made of icing. The dinosaur looked like a crocodile.

Did I imagine that?

No, it really did. I remember how disgusted I felt. I took the cake and threw it into the garbage. I went downstairs to my childhood bedroom and began packing. I was going to finally leave. Not just leave this house. Or this town. Or the coast. No, I was going to just leave altogether. I didn't have any plans for where I would go, but I just knew that I needed to go.

Mom returned home to find a packed suitcase by the front door.

"Oh, did you find another apartment, dear?"

"No."

"Well, I don't want to be nosey, and it is none of my business, but I was just wondering about the suitcase."

"I'm leaving."

"I gathered that. But, where to?"

"I don't know."

I don't think I had ever seen my mother's face look so pale.

"You don't know? But, you can't just go, can you?"

"Of course I can."

"What's your plan?"

"Well, I just purchased a ticket to Paris and I figure once I am in Europe, I'll just hop on trains and head wherever."

"This is a big shock."

"Yeah, it is."

I had a smile on my face that probably worried my mother more than anything else. It was big and goofy, and not at all psychotic.

"How will we contact you?"

"You have my email. I might check it."

"Are you serious about just running away? Is that the answer to your problems?"

I laughed. I laughed in a totally non-crazy way.

"No. Probably not. I don't know if there are any answers, I just think this would be a much better use of my time than lying in bed all day. If I am going to be screwed up, I might as well be screwed up in Prague or Budapest than here."

"I hope it is nothing that we did."

I stopped my frantic frenzy for thirty seconds to give my mother a hug. I wanted to muster up every last shred of warmth and decency I had in my soul and just let her know that I loved her.

"No. It's nothing you've done. But, I have to go."

I left that afternoon and never returned.

Epilogue

Are you tired of post-modern life? Do you have trouble living in the present moment, whether due to traumatic stress, emergency siren annoyance, or chronic illness (non-radiation causes)? Are you frightened about the increasing costs of retirement? Do you remember a time when life seemed simpler? Did you lose your home and loved ones in The Big Quake?

If you answered yes to one or more of the above questions, you may be the perfect client for Grand Pacifica Assisted-memory Stasis Treatment (Grand PAST), a revolutionary service provided by Grand Pacifica Insurance and Health Provision.

For just €250,000 (far cheaper than typical retirement packages), Grand Pacifica will put you into a chemically induced deep sleep, which will be tailored to focus on early, happy memories. You will be able to relive all the highlights of your life before a certain age or event.

Many clients choose to be enrolled in our Millennial Option, a popular feature targeted at members of the age cohort known as "Generation Y" or the "Millennials". In the Millennial Option, clients born between the years 1982 and 2001 are able to focus their Assisted-memory Stasis Treatment around the relatively peaceful turn of the Millennium, when life was simpler and many happy milestones were created.

Grand Pacifica offers loyalty discounts to clients who already hold Grand Pacifica Insurance policies in good standing.

Contact Grand Pacifica today!

Acknowledgements

I guess I need to give a nod to every single person who has crossed my path over the years, no matter how briefly. There may or may not have been a reason for our crossings, but they happened. Perhaps you left a mark on me, and perhaps I on you.

Time
noun /tīm/
times, plural

1. The indefinite continued progress of existence and events in the past, present, and future regarded as a whole

2. The progress of this as affecting people and things

3. The favorable or appropriate *time* to do something; the right moment

4. An indefinite period

5. A more or less definite portion of *time* in history or characterized by particular events or circumstances

6. The conditions of life during a particular period

7. An event, occasion, or period experienced in a particular way

www.ingramcontent.com/pod-product-compliance
Lightning Source LLC
Chambersburg PA
CBHW020637130626
46552CB00003B/1278